THINGS THAT HAVE INTERESTED ME (2S)

CONTENTS

THINGS THAT HAVE INTERESTED ME

W. H. R. RIVERS: SOME RECOLLECTIONS!

It was Siegfried Sassoon who introduced me to this really great swell. He said solemnly: " You must know him. You'll like him." Other young men spoke of Rivers in the same tone. He was a hero of the first order to many. So we met at the Reform Club.

A man of insignificant aspect, small, with a reddish nose indicating an imperfect ability to deal with his waste products. A quiet voice. Capable of silences without self-consciousness. The result of this first meeting was negativeâ as indeed was quite right. Sound friendships rarely begin with violence. I can remember nothing that he said. I noticed only his simple, deep modesty, and that he ate little and drank water, and didn't smoke. My one indictment of Rivers is on the score of his nourishment. I always begin by mistrusting a man who does not enjoy eating and drinking. I recall that

Such was the obscurity of this great man that when these recollections of him were printed in The New Statesman, the editor deemed it prudent to append a footnote explaining who W. H. R. Rivers was I once I got him to drink half a glass of claret and actually to smoke a cigarette. The next day I tried again. " No," he said, "I don't think I'll indulge to-day. I went the pace yesterday."

Then I went to stay with him once or twice amid the fantastically ugly neo-Gothic architecture in the back part of St. John's College, Cambridge, where you lie awake at nights listening to the tinny strokes of multitudinous and absurd public clocks. I saw his bedroom one night. It was very Spartan. The study was large and of agreeable aspect; but he had no genuine interest in domestic comfort, though his ideas about tea were laudable. His study was like a market square. Undergraduates came into it at nearly all hours to discuss the intellectual news of the day. They came for breakfast, but I think that from ten to one he would not have them. During these hours he used his typewriter.

His manner to young seekers after wisdom, and to young men who were prepared to teach him a thing or two, was divine. I have sat aside on the sofa and listened to dozens of these interviews. They were touching, in the eager crudity of the visitors, the mature, suave, wide-sweeping sagacity and experiences of the Director of Studies, and the fallacious but charming equality which the elder established and maintained between the two.

On Saturday nights a discussing society, called the " Socratics," met in his study. I only attended one meeting and it was not a regular, official meeting. I suspect that it was got up for my benefit. In part the proceedings were right over my head, and in part beneath my feet. I have seldom heard wilder intoxicating nonsense talked, and I have never heard more sweet and skilful wisdom from a chairman, nor a more Machiavellian apologetics for the sacred cause of common sense.

Being entirely ignorant of University life, I saw all that Rivers showed me with fresh eyes, and I used to criticise with perhaps undue freedom. The reception of my hasty animadversions by a swell of such dimensions was astounding in its forbearance; on the other hand, my enthusiasm for some of the new instructional methods gave a naive satisfaction to this great man.

I did not really get to know Rivers till he came on board my yacht for a three weeks' cruise. I had gravely warned him that only indiarubber soles were allowed on my decksâ in all other respects he might dress like a Marquesan islander for all I cared. When I met him on the pier at Southampton, lo! he was already wearing tennis shoes.

THINGS THAT HAVE INTERESTED ME (2S)

THINGS THAT HAVE INTERESTED ME (2S)

Arnold Bennett

www.General-Books.net

Publication Data:

Title: Things That Have Interested Me
Volume: 2s
Author: Bennett, Arnold, 1867-1931
Publisher: London : Chatto Windus
Publication date: 1923

Staggered by this excess of zeal, I said: " You don't mean to say you've travelled down in those!" " No," he said, "but I put them at the top of my bag, and changed in the taxi."

I said to myself: " This man is a great traveller."

In the first hour on the yacht he proved that he knew perfectly how to adapt himself to an environment. At intervals he would mention some of the devices he employed on his extraordinary travels in the ends of the earth. He must have been through severe privations. But then, to my mind, all his life was a privationâ or rather a subordination of everything else to his main purpose. He vas a finished adept in the art, which few men of genius or talent acquire in a high degree, of organising his resources and retaining a true perspective.

It was my custom on the yacht to have my morning tea in the deck-house at six-thirty, alone. After a day or two I found him carrying his tea upstairs to join me. He had not suspected that this was my hour for organising my day's work, and that I desired the society of nobody on earth until nine o'clock. I saw that I must make the supreme sacrifice. My virtue of a host was mightily rewarded. Those talks, which occurred every morning, constituted the most truly educational experience I have ever had. Rivers seemed to know something about everything and a lot about nearly everything. If you wanted the name of the unsuccessful candidate at a by-election at Stockport in 1899, he would teu you. But it was less his universal knowledge that impressed me than his lovely gift of co-ordinating apparently unrelated facts. And it was less his gift of co-ordination that impressed me than the beauty, comeliness, and justness of his general attitude towards life.

Also refreshing was the complete absence of conventional replies in his conversation. I said to him: " What infuriates me in you savants is that you do knozu. You have exact knowledge. A novelist is condemned to know nothing about anything." Most people would have replied deprecating such self-abasement and assuring you that really you knew a devil of a lot. Rivers said simply: " Yes, I quite see it's inevitable."

I cannot remember many of his judgments. He criticised Freud freely, but always insisted that he was a great man. On the new Nancy school he was rather cautious; but he mistrusted it. He would say, with an indescribable mild causticity: " I bet you some of those fellows are suggesting things to themselves all day." I broke out once into ferocious strictures upon the confused unreadableness of the final edition of The Golden Bough. To my surprise he agreed in the main, but he would not quite admit that it was a skyscraper built on a supposition. He said the first edition did contain a comprehensible something.

He was thrilling on the subject of the self-protective nature of shell-shock and kindred disorders. A doctor of medicine, he had little belief in current therapeutics. He said, apropos of a recent indisposition: " I thought I'd better call in the magician, and he prescribed something or other. Anyhow, I got better." (All civilised society was a sort of South Sea island to him.) He had a fine, kindly wit, which he used sparingly. He would not say to me: " When's your next novel coming out? " He would say: " When shall we have your next text-book of psychology?"

He read enormously throughout the cruise, assimilating big book after big book, and estimating them as he vvent on. Once he was sea-sick. He just obeyed the tyrannic command and returned to his seat and went on reading. He could read for hours without getting fidgety.

He only failed on one occasion to realise my conception of his imaginative vigour. We went ashore at Torquay, and, contrary to discipline, he left the porthole of his cabin open. A southwest wind arose and kicked up a sudden sea in two minutes, as it will in Tor Bay, and when we got back the bed was soaked through and his dress-clothes also. I supported with fortitude the damage to his dress-clothes, but a bed soaked in salt water can never be used again. Yet the fortitude with which I supported his infelicity was as nothing to the fortitude with which he supported mine. " I have a spare bed on board," I said. " Oh," he said nonchalantly, " that's fortunate! " His imagination had failed to show him that he had been very naughty. As a fact he had little use for beds except as a locus for early morning reflection upon psychological theories.

I thought at first that he had almost no interest in women. But once, when I expressed the view that the segregation of the sexes in University life was a dreadful thing, and that the professed disdainful attitude of undergraduates towards girls was equally deplorable, he surprised me by the candour and warmth of his concurrence. He said the difficulty was to find a way out. He had never been able to think of a way out. He agreed that he himself didn't see enough of women. I said I would give a dance on board for him to look at. It took place on a heavenly evening in the Solent, with a marvellous sunset and the sea as flat as a page of Clement Shorter and as beautiful as a poem by Ralph Hodgson. The young women came off with their cavaliers in canoes and boats. He was fascinated. He said it was something quite strange to himâ in Europe. The young women mistook him for a nonentity. Not one of them had ever heard of him. He enjoyed that. The next morning his remarks on the social phenomenon were price-lessly Marquesan. This was the last real talk I had with him.

This was in a small provincial town where I spent the week-end. There are hundreds of such towns. A beautiful summer afternoon; gentle sun; gentle breeze; beautiful green country around; as good an imitation of summer as you can get in the climate which the Pilgrim Fathers left.

I walked a few hundred yards out of the town; and I saw a football-ground, all complete with goal-posts and miniature grand-stand. It was desertedâ of course. But side by side with the football-ground was a cricket-ground, all complete with smooth pitch and miniature pavilion. And the cricket-ground also was deserted. And side by side with the cricket-ground were tennis-courts, all complete with nets and lines. And the tennis-courts also were deserted. And side by side with the tennis-courts was a bowling-green. And the bowling-green also was deserted.

And the day was the one whole day of the week when the population devoted itself to repose and distraction from work. And quite half the populationâ girls in bright frocks and men with fine necktiesâ was afoot in the dusty roads, strolling aimlessly from nowhere to nowhere, wondering how long it would be to supper-time, and passing and re-passing the deserted cricket-ground and the deserted tennis-courts and the deserted bowling-green.

And with a few exceptions the visible population was visibly stricken with a malady known as boredom. The exceptions sat in modest corners under hedges, and, in pairs, held one another by the waist or by the neck or by the hand.

You see, the grounds and courts and green had been produced with public money. And the population had put the entire management of its public affairs into the hands of a small group of persons whom it had freely elected by secret ballot. This small group genuinely represented the population; and on behalf of the population it had decided and ordained that the health-giving and amusement-giving grounds, courts, and green should not be used on the one day of the week when the population was entirely free to use them.

I walked perhaps a mile farther on, and I beheld dozens of individuals, chiefly belonging to the class which manages the public affairs of populations; and, on superb rolling downs, with lovely glimpses of the sea to give variety to the landscape, they were all enthusiastically playing golf.

No one will believe this astounding story. But it is true.

The unlearned, such as myself, are generally surprised that an ancient and historic university town, such as Cambridge, playing its part well in the great world-drama of the increasing of knowledge, should be provincial. They have an idea that Cambridge ought somehow to resemble a section of central London flourishing in a marsh. But Cambridge is provincial, and must be inhabited, in term time as in vacation, mainly by people whose complacent and attractive provinciality has never been seriously disturbed by contact with a metropolis.

The physical life lived by the inhabitants of Cambridge, and particularly by members of the University, amazes the visitor. The climate is merely infernal. Some of the primary domestic dispositions are still barbaric. The streets are dangerous to anybody who does not happen to be an athlete or an acrobat. Select and recondite diversions are advertised across the thoroughfares in a way which would befit the galas of the Ancient Order of Rechabites in the industrial north. The explorer may discover re-unions of tremendous scholars and educationists deciphering green-tinted newspapers by the aid of candles because they perceive something offensively modern in electric light. The anti-feminist bias is rampant and proud of itself. Manners are hearty, and much resemble those of the Five Towns. " Mind your toes! " cry loudly and cheerfully and callously the late-comers as they crush past you between two rows of stalls in a theatre. And so on. It is curious that in this morally bracing provincial environment there should occur one of the most remarkable examples of perfect and total artistic decadence that England can show. I refer to the performance of " the Greek play."

Of course, the institution of the Greek play can be, and should be, considered with due regard to the principle of relativity. So considered, it is, at any rate in its latest manifestation, rather more than respectable. The mere enterprise is enormous; no spectator not professionally connected with the stage can realise how enormous it is and how well the producers have succeeded. Seeing that my notions of Greek literature are limited to the conviction that Plato is a damned unequal author, and that Professor Gilbert Murray's graceful transmogrifications of Euripides are most ingeniously un-Greek, I would not presume to criticise the Oresteia of Eschylus. I came to it with a mind unimpaired by knowledge, and found that its story is very fine, and full of admirable material either for a Russian ballet or a Famous Players-Lasky film. I also found in it, to my astonishment, the too pure milk of the word of reprisals. I feel sure that if Cam- bridge were under martial law, and Sir Hamar Greenwood had had leisure, the entire chorus would have been slaughtered on the ground that they were in the vicinity of the scenes of the crimes.

The play was under-acted. Such timid acting as obtained was necessarily amateurish, but it achieved consistency and dignity; strangely enough, it was most successful in the women's rolesâ Clytemnestra, Electra, Cassandra. (In this connection I should mention that I addressed a programme-girl in fancy-dress in those deferential tones which one employs towards a society woman who is graciously helping a charity matinee, and not until some minutes after I had bought the programme did I comprehend that I had handed a shilling to a fellow-man.) The music was good and well played, and it was accurately synchronised with the action. The scenery and costumes surpassed the creditable. The choruses were magnificent. They were not professional, but out of sight better than professional, and their work constituted a triumph for Dr. Wood and Mr. Ord. If, as I am informed, Mr. J. T. Sheppard was the supreme adapter, energiser, autocrat, and panjandrum of the affair, he deserves the warmest congratulations. He did not produce simply a drama; he produced an artistic ensembleâ which is a rarity. The effort was colossal; the vision, the diplomacy, the industry that must have gone to it were remarkable, and the final result, allowing for the raw material of it, was in a high degree laudable. So much for the Greek play in its relativity".

But it is far more important to consider the show absolutely. Doubtless the Oresteia is a masterpiece. Doubtless it is one of the chief masterpieces of occidental antiquity. Doubtless there are sound historical reasons why it should bulk so large in our general view of dramatic literature. But that it should be given with so much solemnity, and at such expense of wit and work, in a leading university, is not to my mind a demonstration of taste. To say that it is performed in Greek is to play with words. It is performed in a spoken medium which a tiny majority of persons residing on a small island lying off the western coasts of Europe have agreed among themselves shall be called Greek. Nobody not brought up at an English public school could even seize the mere words, and of the people brought up at English public schools probably not more than 'oi (likelier ooi) per cent, could seize the mere words. If schylus himself could have sat in the New Theatre, Cambridge, he would hardly have guessed that his own work was being performed. The Vice-Chancellor would have had to break it to him gently. The sounds of the words were not Greek, the timbre of the voices was not Greek, nor the emphasis, nor the intonations, nor the vocal rise and fall of the sentences. They could not have been.

As for the beauty and grandeur of the content and of the style, the word-associations which are so intimately and subtly an ingredient of style, the psychological springs of the conduct of the characters, the ideals animating the characters, the attitude of the author towards his antique subjectâ all these things must escape all but the most minute minority of even the most carefully picked audience. The plays are not performed either in the Greek way or in the Greek spirit, and no pretence is made that they are so performed. They could not possibly be so performed. As for the scenery and costumes, what vould schylus have thought of them?

Nine performances were given of the Oresteia. I do not suppose that in all there were nine spectators possessing at once the erudition and the terrific force of imagination necessary to see in, or to see " into," the show the qualities which the ancient Greeks saw in the work as originally performed. A few more persons would, by dint of auto-suggestion, persuade themselves that they saw Greek beauty in the performances.

For the rest of the pleased spectators, in so far as they saw anything but a circus, they were the wiuing victims of a vast hetero-suggestion of beauty. They got something, some conception of the rude curves of the heroical story, but nothing at all commensurate with the mental and physical cost of the production.

If the Greek play is the expensive hobby of an ardent cenacle, well and good. I like expensive hobbies. If it is a link with the pre-electric past, well and good. If it strengthens the co-hesiveness of the social organism, well and good. But as a form of artistic activity it must be judged to be of the last futile decadence, and it denotes a decadence of taste on the part of all concerned. The spirit of Aubrey Beardsley was robust and ingenuous sanity compared with the spirit which renders possible the presentation of this immense archaeological fantasia calling itself Greek.

You come out wondering whether the united ingenuity of a university could not indeed devise something both more educative and more diverting than the Greek play, something less of a blague and of a mystification. The streets of Cambridge seem curiously sane and sound to you. And in the streets there are mighty and peculiar souls that veschylus would have handled had he had the sense to be born into an age of electric light.

"Who in the name of Zeus can that be? " one innocently inquires. And the crushing response comes:

Right perspective is resumed. Before that legendary figure the Greek play dwindles to a storm in a tea-cup.

A LAD and a girl, aged now seventeen and nineteen, committed a crime some time ago and were sentenced at Leeds to twelve and fifteen months hard labour. The case was not reported, and nothing would have been heard of it if the criminals had not appealed, and if the Lord Chief Justice had not had the sagacity to stretch the law and allow the reporters (though not the public) to stay in court while the appeal was heard.

For the criminals were brother and sister; their crime was incest; and, according to the law, incest trials must be heard in camera; that is, they must he hushed up. Why incest trials should be hushed up while sodomy trials and the most sordid divorce trials may be reported in full, I do not know. But I know that judges themselves object to the hushing up of incest trials and wish the ridiculous law altered.

It ought to be altered. The public (like women-jurors) should be ready to face unsavoury facts. In any case I would sooner the public be outraged than kept in ignorance. Secrecy always promotes injustice, oppression, abuses. In the present instance the lad and the girl did undoubtedly commit a crime against society. But that they realised the seriousness of the crime I cannot believe; the Bench admitted that they had been the victims of vile housing conditions, and deserved pity.

Monstrous, iniquitous, and shameful it was that these immature and ignorant young people should be sentenced to the horrors of hard labour, and thereby no doubt ruined for life, because they yielded to a moment's temptation â temptation to which they ought never to have been exposed, temptation for which society itself is to blame. The Appeal Court reduced the sentence to six months without hard labour. It would have been nobler to set the prisoners free.

A philosopher once said: " The price of liberty is eternal vigilance." I will add: " The price of justice is eternal publicity."

In making a play the chief person is the author (though not all producers think so); but the play is only one ingredient of the theatre, and therefore the theatrical manager is the chief person in the sublime institution of the stage. Probably nobody but Sir Hall Caine would dispute this statement.

There are several kinds of manager. There is the favourite of the public, who suddenly takes it into his (or her) headâ a head swollen by innumerable nights of modesty-destroying, open applauseâ that to be under a manager is beneath his dignity. He gets a theatre and two thousand rose-coloured paragraphs of gossip; he issues a programme of brilliant intentions that could not be executed in a dozen years. And in about six months (or less), through the fault of everybody but himself, he is compelled by circumstances to retire from management.

Considering that he has had no training in management, and possesses no gift for management (unless a great talent for occupying the centre of the stage is such a gift), the result never surprises the judicious.

Still, the result is a fine waste of good theatres and of good money.

Then there is the highbrow gentleman who combines some working knowledge of the theatre with a praiseworthy ambition to regenerate the theatre. He ascends the throne with a scorn at once bland and devastating of that abject being, the " commercial manager."

But as soon as he has had a failure (or even before) he gets the wind up, and produces a perfectly footling popular play which fails to be popular. His policy lacks continuity. The public is confused, and the sacred cause of high-browism receives a set-back.

Finally, there is the commercial manager; there is even that abominable concatenation, the commercial syndicate.

Well, after exciting adventures in the theatre for twenty years, I vote for the commercial manager or syndicate every time. Among other virtues the commercial manager has the virtue of not telling you that between gentlemen a written contract is unnecessary. And he has a definite, unchanging policyâ the same policy as Shakespeare had. His aim is to please the public. Also, he knows the mechanics of his job, or, if he doesn't, he employs people who do.

One of his defects is his enormous and contented ignorance of dramatic literature and of the arts in general. Heaven knows that publishers have carried artistic ignorance to a high pitch, but in this respect commercial managers leave them standing. The whole theatre breathes in a thick fog of suffocating ignorance.

Another defect is a marvellous lack of curiosity. Another defect is a deep, natural instinct to refuse plays. Another defect is a tendency to ask for something new while insisting that the something new shall be precisely like every successful play that ever was. Another defect is a firm resolution to sit still in his office and wait for Providence to deposit good stuff on his desk, instead of going out to find good stuff, as editors, publishers, and other merchants do.

But the commercial manager's worst defect is a lack of imagination.

He reads a play, but he has not sufficient imagination to picture to himself what the play will be like when acted on the stage. Managers are continually being astounded when they see the effect on the stage of plays which they themselves have refused.

The defect is almost universal. The secret of theatrical success is the right choice of plays. Not one manager in ten is fitted to choose a play. If the stage is not absolutely perfect, here is one of the chief explanations.

More lies, polite lies, are told about the theatre than about any subject on earth. Only dramatists are excepted from the conspiracy, and even dramatists, when they have had twenty years' success without once producing anything to upset ancient sentimental ideas, seldom hear the truth about themselves in the popular Press. As for managers and actors, they are incapable of doing wrong. If they fail, the fault is always the fault of the public, or the fault of the author, or the fault of the movies, or the fault of ill-luck, orâ most importantâ the fault of the financial situation.

The financial situation of theatres is difficult, but not more difficult than that of other industries. Theatre rents have enormously risen, but so have business rents.

Theatrical accommodation is far too limited, but so is business accommodation. The notion that the theatre is being ruined by a gang of sinister bloodsuckers who lurk mysteriously behind the stage strikes me as abundantly comic. In other industries, faced with a rise of loo or 200 per cent in manufacturing costs, no manufacturer would dream of parting with his goods to the public at the old prices. At present the stage represents a bargain sale to which the public is invitedâ not for one week in January, but all the year round. Theatrical managers are manufacturers. When it occurs to them that, like other manufacturers, they are subject to economic laws, and not living under a regime of heavenly miracles, then the financial situation will begin to look up.

I shall be toldâ perhaps with kindly disdainâ that I do not know what I am talking about. To that criticism only the future can furnish the final answer. And the nature of the answer which the future will furnish can be predicted with certainty. The price of theatre seats will go upâ unless the old axioms that two and two make four, and that you cannot pour two pints and a gill out of a quart-pot cease to be true.

Some will say that theatre seats are a luxury. Well, they are. But the price of every other luxury has gone up. Even the price of books has gone up. True, the book market has been depressed, but not more so than the rubber market, or the cigar market, or the hotel market.

Theatrical managers have combined, not without success, against actors and actresses, against authors, and against stage hands.

Why should they not combine against the public? Everybody else has combined against the public. Politicians do it constantly with brilliant success. Newspaper proprietors have done it to perfection. Tobacco manufacturers do it. All other manufacturers do it. And they do it because they know that the public is a very human monster afflicted with the vice of never paying more than it is compelled to pay.

If the public can amuse itself while sending theatrical managers to ruin, it will assuredly do so, for it has no conscience, but a hard common sense. The public will hear unmoved that a theatre ought to be able to pay its way, and formerly could pay its way, when the weekly receipts amounted to half the weekly holding capacity, and that this is no longer by any means true. Its laughter at a light comedy will be quite untinged by melancholy at this grievous information. The public is heartless, and will yield only to force; but to force it will yield.

Why, then, do managers continue to hope that two and two will soon make three? Because they are afraid of facts, and because they lack faith in their own waresâ in the mighty attraction of the stage.

No names will be mentioned.

The acting profession is a unique profession. All artists have to exploit their individualities, but only entertainers have to exploit their individualities in public. This means that acting attracts the kind of individuality that loves self-. exhibition. It means also that the entertainer, if any success comes at all, is daily subjected to the dangerous ordeal of receiving open and often indiscriminate applause. Entertainers therefore usually begin by being ingenuous and end by being still more ingenuous.

Further, constant contact with the public causes constant exhilaration, which reacts beneficially on the temperament, and even on the health.

Lastly, entertainers must work while the rest of mankind reposes, and repose while the rest of mankind works; which necessarily cuts them off to a large extent from the rest of mankind. It is inevitable that the acting profession should stand by itself, but in this fact there is nothing which needs apology.

No profession works harder while it works, and no profession works more enthusiastically. The keenness of many actors and actresses at rehearsals is prodigious and indefatigable. (Also some of them are very anxious to learn.) The freshness of actors and actresses after a year's monotonous run is equally prodigious. Nine hundred and ninety-nine out of every thousand actors and actressesâ all except a few starsâ do their level best on nearly all occasions. I doubt whether this can be said of any other profession.

And actors and actresses are not commonly-venal. They think of their art first and of money second. A feature of the age is the play-producing society whose aim is entirely uncommercial. Such societies are always springing up. The bulk of the work in them is done by actors and actresses whose extraordinary devotion merits high esteem. That these actors and actresses may have a mixed motive is beside the point. All human motives are mixed motives.

Nevertheless the present is not an age of supreme acting. Supreme acting involves supreme individualitiesâ individualities powerful enough to impose themselves universally on the public. None such is now apparent. We have some fine actors, distinguished actors, clever actors; but not one with native force tremendous enough to become a public legend. (This statement, by the way, does not apply to the musical comedy-revue branch of the profession, in which are several stars each of whom supports the whole organism of a theatre on his shoulders, and has grown legendary.)

And too often celebrated actors will only act themselves. Instead of acting, they are content to exploit their individualities at the expense of the part which they are playing. They seem to want to be recognised instantly as themselves. An ageing actress in a certain play said: " My father could act a railway engine." Actors nowadays have little ambition to act railway engines. And here the actor is not alone at fault; the public also is to blame, for it has unquestionably shown a disposition to frown when favourites appear as anything else than themselves.

What is true of actors is still more true of actresses. Actresses are more amateurish than actors. A few impose themselves considerably by beauty, charm, grace, industry, sincerity; but no star actress stands quite supreme by sheer acting. In one or two instances attempts have been made by small bands of young critics to lift a leading lady into a legend. The attempts have failed, rightly. Even in the musical comedy-revue branch, how often do we see the two chief roles filled respectively by an absolutely great comedian and a charming young creature! It is a common saying in managerial offices, after the male roles in a piece have been satisfactorily discussed: " Yes, but where shall we find the leading actress?"

On the other hand, secondary female roles are frequently filled to perfection. We possess a large number of actresses who can play secondary-roles with really remark-able skill, force, fire, poetry, imagination. You would think they could accomplish simply anythingâ until you put on them the terrific responsibility of a leading role.

No names have been mentioned.

There are too many actors and actresses who can at any rate do their job capably; but there are not enough playwrights. I have spoken of the dearth of leading ladies. It is nothing compared with the dearth of even capable plays.

The notion that good plays are being kept off the stage in large numbers by the blind stupidity of managers is absurd. Very few good plays are being written. The average play submitted to managers is merely imbecileâ inferior even, for example, to the average novel submitted to publishers.

Further, the attitude of the dominant serious playwrights of the time is unfortunate. Is the theatre their sole love? Do they live in and for the drama alone? They do not. With nearly all of them the theatre is or was an afterthought, or at best one of several equal thoughts. Their attitude may be roughly illustrated in the phrase, "Hello! Here is the stage! I ought to be able to do something with it. I've succeeded in other lines of action and I'll try this."

Barrie was a famous novelist before he was a famous playwright. Shaw was a social reformer, novelist, and critic. Galsworthy was and is chiefly a novelist. Yeats was and is a lyric poet. Masefield is a novelist and poet. St. John Ervine was and is a novelist. Maugham was and is a novelist. Lennox Robinson was and probably-still is a manager. Granville Barker was an actor, manager, and producer. Ian Hay was and is a novelist. Scarcely one practising dramatist of any distinctionâ one practising dramatist whose work would be looked at twice by connoisseurs â who devotes the whole of his talent and energy to writing plays! Nay, scarcely one who does not condescend towards the theatre!

This is bad for the theatre. It must be bad. What I want to see is a serious dramatist for whom writing plays is a whole-time job, who has an undivided passion for the theatre. Only by such men will the theatre be restored to its proper position.

I do not know precisely what the drama needs, but I know that it needs something drastic doing to it. Among other treatments, it needs an operation for cataract, enabling it to see the profusion of interesting subjects to which it still remains pitifully blind.

And the rusty fetters of its old-fashioned technique should be struck off with ruthless blows. Looking around, I fail to perceive the doughty figures who might conceivably thus liberate and enlighten the drama.

I do not say that a few good and goodish plays have not been written during this century. But the men who wrote them are no longer very young; they will probably never do better than they have done; and most positively they will never take active part in a genuine renaissance. Who is to replace themâ to say nothing of superseding them? It may be true that a man over fifty has lost the capacity to appreciate really original talent, and therefore I have no right to assert the absence of good new men. But the young themselves cannot see much hope. There is no new dramatist of to-day who divides amateurs of the theatre into two camps. Not one!

I walk up and down the West End, and what do I behold? I behold from The White-headed Boy that Lennox Robinson is progressing. I behold that Hastings Turner has original wit and inventiveness. I behold that the beginner, Reginald Berkeley, has a delightful gift for drawing characters. Well, so far so good. But before my pessimism is dispelled I shall have to see a vast deal more than that. The fact is, this is not a dramatic ageâ anywhere in the world. The German theatre is perhaps the least unpromising.

We had a great dramatist, Synge. He went and died young. It was a greater tragedy than any! that his pen wrote.

All dramatic criticism in morning papers is thoroughly unsatisfactory, and necessarily so, because the conditions under which it is done are impossible. The blame does not lie on the critics, but on the directors of newspapers and the directors of theatres jointly. No critic, however expert, can do justice either to himself or to a play in the time placed at the disposal of critics of morning papers.

The conditions ought to be altered, and could be altered.

In the old days a French daily had three theatrical writers: the " courrieriste," who wrote the gossip; the " soiriste," who wrote a little essay descriptive of the first night, to be printed the next morning; and the critic proper, whose considered opinions appeared once a week. It may or may not be true that the modern public will not wait for tidings of a new play any more than it will wait for reports of a political debate or a divorce case. I doubt if it is true, but even if it is true the difficulty of time might be overcome by sending the critics to the dress-rehearsal of a play.

I remember that at the dress-rehearsals of the Savoy operas the theatre used to be full, and that many critics were among the audience. Moreover, to-day, if a play is produced on Satur- day night, you will often find many of the critics of the Sunday papers at the dress-rehearsal on Friday night. This is the answer to the argument that to send critics to dress-rehearsals would not " work." It actually does " work " when it is tried. And critics, if they chose, might go to both the dress-rehearsal and the first night.

The situation of the critics of evening papers is bad, but not so bad as that of their morning colleagues. And, on the whole, their articles are assuredly better. The articles of the critics of weekly papers are, out of sight, better still.

But a critic needs something else besides time. He needs taste, knowledge, and experience. Very few critics, and especially very few daily critics, possess these three. Many possess the third, some possess the second (usually combining it with an infallible partiality for the tenth-rate), and scarcely any possess the first.

There is one outstanding instance of a critic on the morning Press who is amply provided with all three; but for long years he has refused to take the theatre seriously, and I will not say he is wrong.

As regards daily papers of vast circulation,

I would not demand that critics should express or should even hold opinions that will stand the test of time. No! Big publics prefer that their papers shall reflect their opinionsâ and why not? â and I would be content if morning critics expressed clearly and interestingly what is likely to be the view of the average man about a play.

But they do not. Again and again you will find the most ridiculous plays treated as masterpieces, triumphs, and marvelsâ and the plays fail abjectly. The public has shown more discernment than the critics.

On the other hand, though less often, great popular successes begin their careers amid a chorus of newspaper damns. Thus not seldom the morning critics indicate to the public neither what it will like nor what it ought to like. The fact is that the critics have no discoverable standard.

All that can be affirmed with certainty is that any production, unless it shows real originality, stands a good chance of being grossly overpraised.

I have one additional minor point. Critics might be better employed than in collecting interminable rumours concerning theatrical projects, many of which never m. aterialise. We have arrived at such a pass that more is printed about what theatres intend to do than about what they do do.

Mr. a. B. Walkley's mind is a citadel. He takes in the dead and neatly embalms them; he has also received a few choice aged persons, who are allowed to wander about amid the odours of dissolution; but he has always, and with success, resisted every attempt on the part of anyone under seventy to get inside the citadel. Not very long since, the rumour spread that it had fallen to a comparatively young man. This was not at first credited. Nevertheless it was true. Mr. Walkley published the terrible fact that the citadel had ceased to be virgin. He who had passed thirty-live years in telling the British public what he did not like and could not stomach, blandly stated that he liked the work of Marcel Proust. (True, M. Proust is not a playwright, and Mr. Walkley is mainly concerned with the drama.) M. Proust, by means of endless and serpentine sentences, capable of moving in several directions at once, had insinuated his ways into the citadel, and Mr. Walkley had surrendered. The strangest rape in the historv of criticism! Unhappily M. Proust, doubtless affected by having achieved the impossible, became all of a sudden unreadable. Though his later works sell in considerable numbers, he now has only one reader, Mr. Walkley. Other people buy the books as curiosities, not as matter for perusal.

If you ask why the annals of Mr. Walkley's mind should be of general interest, the answer is that Mr. Walkley has prestige; he has enormous prestige. He has made this prestige. Therefore he is somebody. Nincompoops may acquire popularity, but never prestige. He is the leading English dramatic critic. His prestige, however, needs to be defined. To the " great " public he is unknown. The great public has never heard of him; and if by accident it should attempt to read him, it would impatiently wonder what on earth he was talking about. The theatrical world, and especially actors and actresses, detests him. The theatrical world likes to be liked, and Mr. Walkley dislikes liking. (He once confessed, indeed, that he could hardly bear to see himself quoted in praise of anything. He is as ashamed of praising as some writers are of grammatical infelicities.) Moreover, he disapproves and contemns with suavity, with superiority, and through a microscope: which the sensitiveâ and the theatrical world is nothing if not sensitiveâ must find hard to bear. Mr. Walkley antagonised the theatrical world in the nineties by his use of a single phrase. After the admission that the work of such and such an actor or actress in a play was not entirely revolting to a man of taste, he would add: " The rest were as Heaven made them." I have myself seen the darlings of the gods rendered impotent with pain and fury by this quite undeniable assertion. Just as men of science seek vainly a cure for cancer, so do the ornaments of the stage vainly seek a cure for Mr. Walkley.

Nor does Mr. Walkley's prestige extend to the small world whose inhabitants are inspired by genuine taste and genuine enthusiasm for the theatre and genuine knowledge of the theatre. These rare individuals recognise him only as an upholder of certain traditions which need no support, and as a soul which has never recovered from its first childlike delight in the definition of criticism as " the adventures of a soul."

Where then does Mr. Walkley's prestige reside and reign? It resides and reigns in the facile, refined world of half-educated dilettanti, amateurs, dabblers, and quidnuncs who have the courage of other people's opinions, the cowardice of their own opinions, and the self-protective conviction that in the arts the path of safe criticism is the path of superior disdain. A large world, a busy and restless world, a world deprived of authentic emotion, a world actuated in all its judgments by the secret fear of praising the wrong thing! Mr. Walkley is somewhat better than his kingdom, but he rules in it, and nobody cursed with enthusiasm, originality, and catholic taste could possibly rule in it. If any-such person assumed the sceptic he would be dethroned with contumely in a fortnight. Mr. Walkley's admirers constitute a living demonstration of his second-rateness.

Contrary to the general belief, Buifon did not say that the style is the man. All the same, the style is the man. And Mr. Walkley's style is the man. It may be called dainty, reasonably elegant, though it is never beautiful nor distinguished. Most often it is finicking. It has no verve, no colour, no variety, no daring. One infallible mark of the second-rate is the cliche. Mr. Walkley's compositions are a mass of clichesâ perhaps not the cliches of to-day, but the cliches of thirty years ago. Among the more exasperating of his cliches is, "We are old-fashioned enough to think." And English cliches do not suffice him. His command even of English cliches is so imperfect, so inadequate to serve the ravenous imitativeness of his mind, that he is continually driven to employ foreign cliches alsoâ French, Greek, and Latin. All his articles are thickly encrusted with tags and cliches in various languages, inserted not wholly from ostentation, but partly because he does not know enough English to be able to do without them.

And he indulges immoderately in quotation. Quotations are his lifebelts whenever he has got fhE DRAMATIC CRITIC out of his depth; and he chooses them from a very small number of authors, thus naively proving the limitations of his reading and the impoverishment of his ideas.

At one time he could scarcely write a criticism without bringing into it the Dickensian " All werry capital." And I doubt whether Mr. Walkley with his " all werry capital " is more acutely distressing than the feeblest of dramatic critics who will say, for instance, that an actor " did yeoman service " in a performance. The one falls just as far as the other below the level of the style, unaffected and vigorous, of, say, Mr. St. John Ervine, who has something individual to express and always expresses it with the minimum of fuss.

"Sturdy " may seem an odd epithet to apply to Mr. Walkley. Yet he is sturdy in one thing â his provincialism. And to charge him with provincialism may seem odd, too. Yet he has industriously cultivated provincialism for many years. Go into a provincial city and discuss any of the arts, and one of the first remarks to warn you will be: " We're very critical down here! " Talk of your own adventuresâ you will be met with an instinctive hostility, and the conversation will be turned to the adventures of the inhabitants, perhaps twenty or thirty years before; and if you have insight you will perceive the futility of trying to talk about anything else. You will perceive, further, that the inhabitants have labels for everything, and that anything which cannot be fitted with a label does not exist for them and is thereby condemned. This is a survival from the eighteenth century, when the sternest condemnation of a novelty was: " Qa ne ressemhle a rien.

The inhabitants keep an eye, if an inimical eye, on affairs generally. Of some affairs they know a great deal. They can be as refined and as exacting within their circumscribed tasks as any metropolitan. But they demand intellectual and aesthetic stability. They are comfortable. They love their comfort. They will not be robbed of it. And whatever or whoever threatens to rob them of it by means of phenomena to which they are unaccustomed is bound metaphorically to have his head bashed in. They are extremely sensitive, and, like all extremely sensitive people, they are extremely egotistic.

AH which appears to me to apply pretty closely to the case of Mr. Walkley, who has the provincialism not of place but of mind. He may have been born a metropolitan, but he has gradually retired from his original exciting situation. His super-sensitiveness could not stand the tossing of the great tide of evolution. His egotism suffered with his sensitiveness. He had begun to be educated, but the process of real t: he dramatic critic education is rather painful. He put an end to it, preferring to remain half-educated and have peace. He transformed himself into a citadel. The sublime act was accomplished when Bernard Shaw first turned dramatist. Mr. Walkley once explained with sympathy a shattering play of Mr. Shaw's. Having proved his quality, he determined never to renew the feat. He now lives among the embalmed, the enemy of enthusiasms, passions, all emotions, all novelties. His tranquillity must be respected. Even M. Proust, his sole invader, gracefully respects it by writing the same book over and over again, at greater length and with ever-increasing refinement and finickingness.

The most baffling mystery of the age is this: Why did Mr. Walkley take up with dramatic criticism, and why has he never dropped it? Often and often have I beheld the citadel in the stalls on a first night, urbanely smiling, aloof, withdrawn, moveless, disdainful, defying comprehension, refusing all contact. I have speculated intensely upon the possible clues to the enigma. And there has come into my head a queer suspicion, to which I attach little importance, that Mr. Walkley surveys the modern stage as a spiritual exercise to test his powers of repudiation. At any rate he fulfils a useful function in an epoch where any treacly mess of senti- mentality is liable to be acclaimed in print as " a great play at last." A critic who is adamant to all modern manifestations, though he may never praise what is original, will certainly never gush over what is bad. That is something; it is a corrective which we need.

Which is you.

Of course, sometimes you are not yourself. As at a first night, for example. You are professional then, or interested by professional or other ties in the performance, or you attend through a desire to be in the swim. I would sooner have any audience than a first-night audience.

When you are yourself you are never professional, and you have no interest whatever except to be entertained; you are, however, generally a little bit snobbish, for a mild degree of snobbishness is inherent in almost every human being. The great difficulty which you present is that you are not demonstrative. The majority of you go to the theatre and are pleased or displeased, and leave the theatre without giving a sign of your state of mind.

The poorest joke will raise a laugh in the theatre, and if a dozen people laugh any individual is inclined to conclude that the audience is amused. But the average Briton seldom laughs in a theatre when he is amused. He may smile. He may do nothing at all, and yet be amused. When the majority of an audience laughs, either the action of the play is held up or a number of lines are not heard. A play may be punctuated by the laughs of a few and yet fail. A play may be received with apparent indifference and yet succeed. And as with humour, so with pathos.

A hundred persons well distributed in an audience of a thousand can, and often do, produce an air of success which may be quite illusory. What many professionals live and die. without perceiving is that applause comes from a tiny minority of you. Let anybody during what is termed " loud applause " look round at the audience. He will see that the majority of you are offering no manifestation of feeling. I have never heard such miagnificent genuine applause as during the Gilbert and Sullivan seasons at the Princes Theatre. It gave me a new conception of what eager and sane applause can be. But I estimated that even then not more than 60 per cent, of you were applauding.

No! You are not demonstrative. That is one reason why you are so puzzling. But it is not a fault. I suppose you have faults. They are the faults of humanity. The instinct of self-protection causes you to be hostile towards anything that is really new; it might upset your ideas, make you think, weaken the structure of society. You naturally don't want that. And you are too easily satisfied with the mediocre, and your appreciation of beauty is not very sensitive.

But for myself I should as soon dream of finding fault with the law of gravity as with the public. You are absolute monarch. A horse cannot be forced to drink against his will, and you cannot be entertained against your will. It's no use. You are, and that is all there is to it. For us professional entertainers you are the unalterable instrument upon which we have to play. If we cannot please you and ourselves too, why, then, we are lacking in skill. Shakespeare managed to do it. And, like ourselves, you do learn. You move exceedingly slowly, as a leviathan must; but you move. At a performance of the Phoenix Society some time since, I discovered that the Phoenix Society had done quite a lot with you.

Finally, you have a terrible defectâ it is not a fault. You lack artistic keenness. You don't care very much either way. No play, no opera, no picture, and seldom a book, is an " event " in Britain. In Berlin, on a Strauss first night, the papers used to issue special editions after each act. Can you conceive such a phenomenon on this isle?

People admit themselves " unwell" oftener than they used to do. That is because they know a little more about the greatest of all physical marvels and mysteries, the human body. In former days an indisposition was looked upon as the act of God, and regarded fatalistically. Now it is known to be the act of man, and therefore, perhaps, curable if officially proclaimed and treated. The champions of the past in this matter say that we are a generation of mollycoddles; but the champions of the past are usually persons of immensely strong physique, and they take credit to themselves for what has been merely their good luck. Worse, they will attribute their longevity and their good health to some perfectly footling habit.

"I am eighty-five, and have all my own teeth," says a man. " Why? Because I shave after washing. The new generation washes after shaving. If it would only shave after washing " etc.

Still, we live appreciably longer than our ancestors. Some will assert that since life is a nuisance, long life is a still greater nuisance. But if you ask these whether they would be willing to go back to the old state, the answer will either be in the negative or it will be a lie.

In some ways we have retained the foolishness of the past. To-day, just as in the past, there are certain diseases, especially those affecting physical attractiveness, as to which women will unfailingly become hysterical. And men are as apt as ever to become hysterical if their digestive organs go wrong. Also, a person who knows he suffers from a chronic malady will attribute all his ills to that malady, forgetting that he is as liable as his fellows to some scores of other maladies.

On the other hand a man will still as of old deny to himself the existence of an obvious chronic malady, and carry on his existence exactly as if his proper place was not in bedâ and then die suddenly, and have the effrontery to be surprised thereat.

Again, we still dose ourselves as if we had expert knowledge, and swear at doctors. It is true that doctors don't know much about disease, but they know much more than laymen. Our forefathers indulged in what were called herbs and simples. We indulge in pills (of various shapes), and on a far vaster scale. Herbs and simples possibly did some good in a few cases, when used with knowledge and discretion. The same, and not more, may be said of self-administered pills. You can get pills scientifically and admirably prepared to cure any mortal thing short of a broken leg. Nothing can be said against good pills. But much can be said against the ignorant and immoderate users of good pillsâ that is, the great majority of us. Pills form part of the secret life of nearly all of us. We have the vice of drug-taking, and about 95 per cent, of the pills swallowed in a little water serve no good purpose. That they do small permanent harm is due to the tremendous resisting powers of the human organism.

The trade in drugs must be terrific; and though I object to our liberty being stolen from us bit by bit by a Government that is worse than forty thousand grandmothers, I admit that when the British Government prohibited the unfettered sale of certain very dangerous drugs it won my applause. Only yesterday we could walk into a shop and buy as easily as biscuits enough sulphonal, veronal, and trional to ruin the lives of a whole family. This was the liberty to perish, and governments are not entirely vile.

We have not yet arrived at a comprehension of the deep truth that a man who is his own doctor has a fool for his patient. Even doctors rarely treat themselves!

Many, if not most, persons regard a doctor as a magician, and in this respect we have not improved much on the remote past, when magicians were the only doctors. A patient will believe simply anything from a doctor who attended the patient's father and mother. The

"family doctor " is infallible, and no amount of funerals will affect his infallibility. We are like savages in another point, that sometimes we kill our magicians, that is to say, we change our doctors, often for no reason except that we want fresh magic.

In this yearning for fresh magic we are apt to go to " the nearest man," not because the slightest delay might be fatal, but because it is simpler to go to the nearest man. Yes, and it happens sometimes that we choose a doctor because he plays good golf or good tennis, or because his motor-car looks smart, or because his political opinions coincide with our own, or because he takes a dignified part in the public life of the town, or because he has a nice smile.

Most ailments get cured or cure themselves in the end, yet if the new doctor has a nice smile or plays good golf and the first case is a success, then he is unalterably established in our esteem as a magician for years to come.

The fact is that doctors simply are not chosen for their professional skill, and professional skill is only one of the ingredients of a successful medical practice, and not the most important one. Not seldom, indeed, a very successful practice is achieved without any professional skill worth mentioning. At best doctors are chosen for their characterâ and how many of us are sure judges of character? Human nature is D such that the best of us may be deceived by a doctor who is honestly deceiving himself. I knew a doctor who built up a fine practice and a considerable fortune on one method. He was a mediocre physician, but he had the invaluable gift of persuading himself that if he had been called in twenty-four hours later the case might have proved fatal.

"My dear sir, or madam," he would say to a new patient, after the first few days, speaking in a quiet, restrained, and authoritative voice, "I didn't care to speak earlier, but I may tell you now that you called me in only just in time. Another day and I shouldn't like to think what might have happened. However, I was fortunate in my treatment, and the danger is over for the present."

Patients were enormously impressed. At the end of his splendid career that doctor had the conviction that he had positively saved the lives of half the community which he adorned. And he was not alone in the conviction.

The patient will naturally ask: " But how can I judge the professional skill of a doctor? " The answer is that he cannot. To a certain extent the laity is at the mercy of the medicals. But the patient can, at any rate, judge his doctor on the manner in which he approaches the case. The good doctor approaches the case in a spirit of scientific inquiry. The good doctor will not limit his attention to the particular ailment or symptoms which are the occasion of his visit. He will know that an ailment seldom stands by itself. He will inform himself about the patient's age, vocation, daily habits, and medical history, and he will note these things down. Then he will get at the history of the particular ailment, the present symptoms, and, especially, just what made the patient send for him at just that moment. Then he will make a thorough examination of the patient, and, if the case is serious, he will make several examinations. He will consider the patient's physique as a whole and his existence as a whole; and then he will prescribe. He will assuredly not give the impression to the patient that the malady is accidental, or that the treatment consists wholly or even chiefly in bottles of medicine, powders, pills.

If a doctor conducts his professional work in this spirit, with this thoroughness, and with this sense of proportion and of perspective, the chances are that he really knows his job and has the character and ability to execute his job successfully. If he doesn't, then the chances are that, despite good golf, dignified deportment, and a nice smile, he is not a competent doctor according to modern standards. And all these things will count for little unless a diligent attentiveness is maintained. You may say that the most foolish patient would take stock of a doctor's attentiveness or lack of it, and act accordingly. Not always so. I once knew a doctor who said to a patient:

"It is of the greatest importance that you should eat nothing, you understand, nothing, until I have seen you again. Please remember, nothing!"

He called again in three weeks. And this was not uncharacteristic of his ways. Yet he had a big country practice and was beloved as a magician.

Modern clinical standards show some improvement on those of even eight years ago, and for two reasons, both due to the war. In the first place, during the war perhaps five million men either went through hospitals or came up frequently for hospital parade. And despite their frequent dissatisfaction they thereby learnt a very great deal about medicine and medical and surgical treatment. They now know something about what a thorough diagnosis is, and they have spread their knowledge among families and friends. If they fall ill, or if their relatives fall ill, they expect a scientific attitude and some attention to detail from their doctors. They are aware of some of the latest devices, and they are discontented if the said devices are not applied to themselves.

The day is gone when the doctor, on being summoned, could come and chat miscellaneously and pleasantly of nothing in particular for a quarter of an hour, and then glance casually at the tongue for two seconds, take the pulse in thirty seconds, and, murmuring vague reassurances and a promise to dispatch coloured medicine, depart full of complacency and honour.

And in the second place the doctors have learnt a lot. Doctors, including panel doctors, were called up and put under the very best men in all sorts of hospitals throughout the country. Doctors were also attached to medical boards and pension boards. They necessarily acquired precious information concerning the absolute necessity of careful diagnosis according to a routine which omitted nothing, and they returned to their ordinary practices loaded with the said information and habituated to methods of diagnosis and treatment which at any rate are not unscientific. And so the doctor is now more or less able to supply what the enlightened patient demands. Before the war, everybody who was accustomed to both English and French doctors must have been struck by the more searching and thorough methods of the latter. The difference between the two was indeed sometimes quite startling. I do not desire to praise French doctors at the expense of English, and I am entirely convinced that English hospitals, both military and civil, were and are superior to French; but I know from an experience extending over years that the French doctor had at least a scientific attitude towards disease, especially in diagnosis, which was exceedingly rare in the English.

t!.,. io

It seems that poor people who take advantage of the law enabling the impecunious to get divorce cheaply are put at a serious disadvantage because they are poor people. If they have sinned themselves, they must confess itâ and seriously injure their prospects of getting a decree, whereas Court officials are expressly forbidden even to ask rich petitioners whether they have sinned.

This, of course, is scandalously unfair. But it is not more scandalously unfair than lots of other things in our marriage laws. For instance, till quite recently it was scandalously unfair that if you lived in the far provinces and wanted a divorce, you had to come to London and bring all your witnesses to London, and maintain them there in order to get a divorce.

No one need come to London in order to be hanged or to be sentenced to penal servitude for life. Oh no! The State will conveniently arrange that for you in your own district.

It was, until quite recently, scandalous that though you could marry your deceased wife's sister, you could not marry your deceased husband's brother. Church dignitaries prophesied, when you were first allowed to marry your deceased wife's sister, that the permission would mean the end of true home life; and when the deceased husband's brother question came before Parliament, the same prophets prophesied the same dreadful prophecies about that also. But true home life seems still somehow to persist.

All progress towards justice is always impeded. It ought to be impeded a little; but it is impeded too much. The cost of both executive and legislative justice is excessive either in time or in money or in bothâ partly because the lawyers' trade unions are the most powerful in the country, and partly because a grossly overworked Parliament has no time to simplify the ways of justice.

The most disastrous fact in our national life is that we have only one legislative machine.

It results in astounding phenomena. Thus to save trouble Parliament decided, instead of making divorce cheaper, to make the State pay for the divorce of poor personsâ if the poor persons were willing to humiliate themselves sufficiently!

Our judicial system is possibly the finest in the world. But it is tragically expensive. We have one law for rich and poor alike. True! But as a rule the poor can't pay for the law. Luxuries are not for the poor, and our greatest, noblest luxury is the law.

When people say " the shops," they don't mean butchers' shops or bread shops. They mean the shops in which women's attire is the sole or the leading merchandise.

And when they say " the sales," they mean chiefly bargains in women's attire. The shops count amongst the greatest attractions of London and the provincial cities. They draw to their windows enormously larger crowds than Westminster Abbey or the National Gallery. There are half a dozen spots in the West End where the spectacle of shop windows full of frocks, hats, and lingerie results in blocked pavements for several hours every day. No other kind of wares will regularly block pavements. And let it be admitted that no other kind of wares are so pretty and agreeable to look at, and therefore so worthy to block pavements. The richly variegated windows of a big shop, just illuminated at twilight, with the dark upper storeys setting off their brightness, and the hypnotised crowds passing slowly in front of them, make a show that for truly romantic beauty cannot be beaten in London, and I will back it against any sunset seen from Westminster Bridge. Further, sunsets are not improving in elegance, and shop windows are.

And not in the main thoroughfares alone is women's attire the paramount display and lure.

A similar phenomenon is to be observed in the newspapers. You might turn over the pages of a daily and miss the Parliamentary reportâ you could not possibly miss the vi omen's attire. For, quite apart from the immense and comprehensive illustrated advertisements of it, now infinitely more imposing and delightful than in the past, women's attire is treated every day in most papers as a special item of the day's news, with the aid of original designs and photographs. It may be the only illustrated news in the paper. Cricket may shrink, even racing may wither in a drought, but the journalistic importance of women's attire never abates. Newspapers have realised what women's attire has come to mean to the community, but I doubt whether the community itself has yet consciously realised to what a tremendous extent this dazzling subject has captured the general imagination.

Any sensational preacher who lacks a topic for his fulminations can find it, and often does find it, in women's " finery "; any layman who happens, for private reasons, to be out of love with the sex, will try to revenge himself by scarifying women's peculiar folly as demonstrated by the pursuit of fashions; and not for generations have women been more fiercely attacked on account of their clothes than during the last four or five years. According to the attackers, social and religious, the matter is perfectly simple:

Women as a sex are foolish about their clothes, and that is the beginning and the end of it. But I doubt if the matter is so simple.

For example, no man has yet shown that women are more foolish than men in the affair of clothes. Men are slaves to fashion; they allow themselves no latitude. And when they do escape from some unusually fatuous convention, they do what they can to get back to prison, as witness the present grand masculine effort to restore the top-hat to its ancient tyranny. Nor are men any more " practical" than women in their clothes. A human being who will wear black or dark clothes in hot weather would commit any folly. Consider the male waistcoat, which is thinnest in exactly the region where it covers the most sensitive part of the bodyâ the spine! Consider the starched shirt. No, better not consider it! There are objects too shocking, too barbarous, too grotesque for the consideration of nice-minded persons.

As for the relative extravagance of the two sexes in clothes, I am not convinced that the wife's cost on the average more than the husband's. The husband knows as a rule what the wife spends, but unless he is a lunatic he does not disclose to her what he himself spends. A clever woman would conjure half a dozen evening-frocks out of the price of her husband's dress-suit. One of my friends, a misguided statistician, proved to me the other day that every time I don evening-dress I dissipate ten shillings. And, anyway, women array themselves to please men, and because men positively want them to be arrayed, and would be vexed if they were not arrayed. The attitude of men towards women's clothes is perhaps the grossest possible example of hypocrisy, confused thinking, cheap sneering, and downright meanness that the history of the human race can show.

To understand clothes it is necessary to grasp two fundamental truths.

The first is that fashion is not an evil but a good. Fashion is an expression of convention, and conventions are the cement of society, or, to express it otherwise, the essential antidote to anarchy and the main support of order. Fashions exist everywhere, in everything. There are fashions in religious belief, in doctors' prescriptions, in charities; and if there were no fashions in costume the resulting mess would be considerable. Fashions are not confined to highly civilised communities. They are strongest in primitive communities. Take a small island in the Solomon group. It is about a mile across. A line divides it into two parts and into two fashions of attire. On one side of the line the women dress unpractically but decently, on the other they dress practically (with pockets) but indecently.

The second truth to be grasped is that dress is not wholly or chiefly a matter of protection and of decency. The purposes of costume are, and always have been, various. Among them are the desire to attract the opposite sex, to hide blemishes, to disclose or heighten beauties. All which purposes are surely legitimate. And as for ornament, the origin of much personal ornament is magicalâ religious or medicinalâ and some personal ornament still is magical in its intention, seeing that both men and women still wear things " for luck."

Of course it cannot be denied that some women dress principally for display, in order to prove how rich they are or how rich their husbands are. This may be vulgar, but it is not vicious, and if such women dress artistically, as now and then they do, they go far to justify themselves; for if luxury contrives to be artistic it fulfils a proper and important function in the commonwealth. How important the function is you may realise by conceiving the commonwealth without any luxury at all! Luxury meets a universal desire; but it is relative. Everybody wants some luxury, and nearly everybody gets some luxury. The only luxuries that people cavil at are the luxuries which do not happen to appeal to their tastes or which they cannot personally afford to pay for. Each of us looks at the existence of such luxuries as a sign of decadence and decay.

It is notorious that a marked change has come over feminine costume. Modern frocks have been attacked as vulgar, insufficient, shameless; and they are supposed to be an illustration of that " loosening of the bonds " which accompanies a great war. The favourite theory is that in the war women grew hysterical. Tens of thousands of them left their homes for a new freedom, and incidentally enjoyed the disposal of far more money than ever they had before. The feeling of independence, coupled with the sense of the possibility of the break-up of civilisation, was too much for them. Rules of conduct went to smash. Morals were forgotten. Desire ran riot. Modesty expired. Nothing mattered. And the expression of the feminine state of mind was seen in the fashions!.

An interesting, even an exciting, theory, delightfully simple; but it should be received with caution! In the first place the new fashions were beginning before the war; they had certainly begun before women had stepped into the new freedom and before the fear of universal disaster had developed. And in the second place the new fashions came from France, where women, before Englishwomen, had suffered bereavement on a great scale, and where there was no new freedom or independence to make them hysterical or vicious or careless. In fact, the common theory, if it explains the new fashions at all, does so only in an extremely slight degree, and the true, full explanation, when it is worked out, will probably be very much more complicated and very much less theatrical. We are not likely to find the true, full explanation in our time. Meanwhile let usâ and especially those of us who are men or old womenâ be chary in our accusing.

When you have settled in your own mind upon a theory which accounts for the alleged immodesty, indecency, suggestiveness, or whatever you like to call the quality, of the modern frock, the question remains: Is the modern frock immodest, etc. etc.? Some women would manage to be immodest or suggestive, no matter what the fashions might be. But such women in all ages are exceptional, and must be omitted from a general estimate of the situation. These exceptions apart, I do not think that a charge against the morality of the modern frock can be sustained. Assuredly skirts are short, but they have not yet risen to the knees; and after all, what is reprehensible in the short skirt? It is more hygienic; it is more comfortable; it gives greater freedom to those contrivances upon which women walk; it enables them even to run with the said contrivances. And undoubtedly women revel in the new physical freedom. I have an idea that the mentality which regrets the long skirt is the same mentality which in China insisted on rendering women's feet quite useless for ambulatory purposes. Are short skirts suggestive? I should say that they are the very opposite of suggestive.

The other day, in a West End street, I saw a young woman in an uncompromisingly long skirt. Well, it shocked me. I thought: " This young woman must be a peculiar and a perverse young woman. I wonder what is the matter with her?" There came into my mind the celebrated lines of Sir John Suckling:

"Her feet beneath her petticoat Like little mice stole in and out As if they feared the light."

And the lines positively struck me as perverse and suggestive. Why should little feet have to peep in and out, and why should they behave themselves as if they feared the light? I consider that the new fashions have done well to take us beyond the peeping stage and the coy stage and the falsely prim stage. And I should like to have been able to say to the young woman: " Please go home at once and dress yourself decently."

As regards the upper portions of the modern frock, it may for a period have descended too far, but in essentials it never, at its most audacious, went beyond the point demanded by Queen Victoria at her dinner-parties. It is on record that young women guests sometimes had to have their evening-dresses hastily altered within the royal dwelling because the admirable Victoria, beloved of the bourgeoisie, would not tolerate under-exposure of the female body at dinner or after dinner! Probably she hated suggestive-ness. If she did, she would probably have objected to the modern, knitted, high-necked, tight jumper worn without a corset; and yet I have never heard critics of the modern costume utter a word against the tight jumper. Nor have I heard them assert that the modern costume is ungraceful or ugly. The factâ and the most important fact of allâ is that women have not been so becomingly and beautifully dressed for ages as they are to-day.

Naturally all the professional Jeremiahs and Habakkuks, if silenced on their ac- cusation of immodesty or insufficiency in the modern frock, will fasten on the " exaggerated interest " which women, and especially girls, now show in dress, and will charge the sex not only with monetary extravagance in clothes but also with devoting a great deal too much time to clothes. I have already referred to the question of expense. Of one thing I am quite certain, namely, that if the average modern girl spends too much on her frocks, her predecessor of the last generation did not spend enoughâ was not indeed allowed to spend enough. Even to-day, I am inclined to think, the average married woman is pinched in her dress-allowance, so that her career as a wearer of nice frocks is one long series of tucks, devices, dyeings, modifications, and bargain- hunting. In any case I have not the slightest fear of the modern young woman ruining herself or her family by dressing herself too well. That profound spirit of moderation which characterises the British and which again and again brings the country through enormous crises that in other countries would result in revolutionâ that same spirit is always at work in the modern woman, even when she finds herself among a surging crowd of hypnotised and feverish companions in one of those magical palaces which we call shops.

Again, as regards the amount of attention and time bestowed on clothes, I am quite certain that if the modern girl bestows too much of these precious commodities on adornment, her predecessor did not spend enough. A girl can make herself decent and keep herself warm by a quarter of an hour's attention per day to the task. But to dress well is an art and an extremely complicated and difficult art; and the less money you have available for the purpose the more complicated and difficult it becomes. It com- prises all manner of problems connected with the hair, the complexion, the hands, the feet, jewellery, and Heaven knows what else. And above everything it comprises the expression of the individuality. If a woman's attire does not express and enhance her individuality, then it is a failure. And to express one's individuality by means of textiles, at the same time keeping within the fashions, is an affair whose delicacy can be guessed by any man who has ever chosen a necktie " to suit him." I wish that women could see a man hesitating between forty neckties in a hosier's shop. The sight would furnish them with effective retorts when they were next attacked about their gewgaws.

I have called women's dressing an art. To my mind it is the most influential of all the arts, and is capable of giving more pleasure to the community at large than all the other arts combined. It has professors worthy to rank with the foremost painters, musicians, poets, and architects.

Tens of thousands of girls herd themselves into vast institutions in order to learn how to sing or play. In 90 per cent, of the cases the effort comes to absolutely nothing. In a few cases it ends in a concert or a picture and the amiable applause of friends. Perhaps in one case out of a thousand is real talent, capable of giving real general pleasure, produced.

Yet these same aspirants will call themselves serious persons, while despising a girl who devotes herself with a similar passion to her appearance. But a well-dressed woman is giving pleasure all the time; she is exercising a civilising influence all the time. Her show doesn't begin at 8.15 and last for an hour and a half in an enclosed hall. Nor is it necessary to go to the Royal Academy to see what she has accomplished. Her show is a continuous performance. It is private and it is also public. Everybody who witnesses it is, consciously or unconsciously, uplifted by it. It is the finest and the most powerful application of the poetic principle to daily, ordinary life. In a word, every well-dressed woman is a public benefactor. You may call her all the bad names you like, but she is a public benefactor.

One of the greatest living English journalists, who signs himself " Wayfarer " in The Nation, wrote a paragraph about Charles Garvice apropos of the latter s death) which appeared to me unjust. I therefore protested as follows:

"' Wayfarer ' expresses the ignorance of himself and his friends about the late Charles Garvice; and for himself as a famous publicist he quite properly seems rather ashamed of this perfect unacquaintance with an outstanding social phenomenon. He brackets Charles Garvice and Mrs. Florence Barclay together. This he should not do. Charles Garvice had an immensely greater hold on the public than Mrs. Barclay, and for reasons w hich are creditable to both author and public. The work of Charles Garvice has little artistic importance; but he was a thoroughly competent craftsman. He constructed well and wrote clearly and not inelegantly, and he had a certain imaginative faculty. Artistically his novels are at least on a level with scores of novels which have been seriously reviewed in your columns, and with some which people are seriously discussing in circles that deem themselves enlightened this very day. Further, Charles Garvice was utterly free from any sort of snobbery, intellectual or otherwise. Further, both directly and indirectly, by his own freely given energy and skill, he accomplished a very great deal for the improvement of the conditions under which authors vork. ' Wayfarer ' laments the loss of ' that precious thing, a common national standard of good literature." There never was any. Good books, not excluding the classics to which ' Wayfarer ' specially refers, are as highly and widely esteemed to-day as ever they wereâ probably more so."

"Wayfarer " acce-pted this-protest so far as it concerned Charles Garvice, while maintaining his general position; but Mr. Middle ton Murry, who surely ought to occupy the throne once occupied by Nicholas Brakespeare, retorted grandiosely. Among other things he wrote:

"Whether there ever was a common national standard of good literature I do not know. It does not necessarily follow from the fact that Scott, Byron, and Dickens were immensely popular in their dayâ far more popular, for instance, than Mr. Wells is in ours. But if this fact does not prove that there was a common national standard then, it does prove that the popular writers of a hundred years ago had infinitely more artistic, literary, or social conscience than they have to-day."

Part of my reply to Mr. Middleton Murry ran thus:

"I may be too fond of emphasising the mechanical element in the profession of literature. But I wish to heaven some of my contemporaries would emphasise it a little more. The English, however, seem to have a distaste for thorough technical competence in literature. They have not yet got rid of the Byronic attitude.

"I admire Mr. Murry's courage in asserting that ' the popular writers of a hundred years ago had infinitely more artistic, literary, and social conscience than they have to-day." (Mr. Middleton Murry's Englishâ an example of what scorn of the mechanical' element leads to!) He specially mentions Byron, Dickens, and Scott. Byron was a great genius. Do7i Juan is a terrific work. But there is scarcely a page of it which does not show that an artistic conscience was not Byron's strong point. It is notorious that Dickens, like Thackeray, often wrote under self-imposed conditions (especially conditions of haste) which made real artistic integritv impossible. The same is even more true of Scott. Nearly everybody knows this, and if Mr. Murry does not know it he should acquaint himself with literary history, and so for the future avoid making generalisations which are en- tirely absurd.

"Not long since I re-read Quentin Durzvard. What a book of hasty expedients, adroit evasions of difficulties, and artistic ' slimness'! If I wasn't so tragically addicted to money-making I would write a destructive study of Quentin Durward. And, incidentally, I would prove that the ' artistic, literary, or social conscience' is quite as active to-day as ever it was.

"Mr. Murry says that he can sympathise with my ' evident desire to disconcert the preciousness of the aesthete." But when he says that things such as Charles Garvice made were ' simply not worth making well," etc., I charge him with precisely the preciousness of the aesthete. Was it not worth while to give pleasure to the naive millions for whom Charles Garvice catered honestly and to the best of his very competent ability? Ought these millions to be deprived of what they like, ought they to be compelled to bore themselves with what Mr. Murry likes, merely because Mr. Murry's taste is better than theirs? The idea is ridiculous. The idea is snobbish in the worst degree. Taste is still relative. Mr. Murry, though his recent services to the cause of good taste in all the arts have been conspicuously brilliant and laudable, has probably not yet reached the absolute of taste. Charles Garvice's work was worth doing, and since it was worth doing it was worth doing well."

Hyde Park â 6.30, on a Tuesday night In February.â A girl was preaching. She had seven or eight official supporters, including an old man and a young man and two nice-looking girls much younger than herself. The preacher " held forth "â no other phrase would serve as wellâ in a strident voice, and with gestures both monotonous and violent, to a numerous crowd. She had nothing whatever to say except: " Seek God," and she made no smallest attempt to explain the nature or the method of this highly mystical affair of seeking God. The formula seemed to satisfy her.

She was one of those speakers who cannot stop. They want to stop; they would give a great deal to stop; but they are victimised by a secret inhibition against stopping.

She tried again and again. Over and over she repeated the evening chaplet of cliches. She was like an ant, or some other of Fabre's insects, walking endlessly round the rim of a vase. At last by accident she fell off. Another girl handed her cloak to her, but she was too preoccupied and enchanted to put it on, despite the cold. Then this other girl began to preach. But neither of the pretty girls preached. The old man, hatless in the chilly breeze, kept ejaculating at intervals,

"Praise God " and " Amen." The tedium of the performance was intense.

More interesting was another group, at the core of which two men were arguing upon God. One of them had just been preaching, and now he was being tested. They argued in quiet, reasonable tonesâ indeed, so quietly that only the half-dozen people nearest them could hear what they said. The rest of the attentive crowd craned their necks in vain to catch wisdom. The debaters were magnanimous one to another. Evidently their aim was not victory but truth. Said the preacher handsomely:

"Of course don't know everything. don't know all God's plans. Even Christ didn't."

The argument proceeded for a long time, and the unfed crowd went on hoping for crumbs and not getting them.

Close by, a smaller congregation listened to the polite contentions of two aged men who were smoking cigarettes. Again the same quiet, reasonable tones, as of intellects well able to handle the most majestic and exciting themes without any inward disturbance. I heard one question:

"Well, then, what do you call the thing that thinks? Do you call it the brain?"

But the wind and the dull roar of Oxford Street traffic withheld the answer from me.

Being favourably situated for visits to Hyde Park, I have joined congregations on scores and scores of occasions, and have always been disappointed. I am convinced that the leading characteristic of the majority of the preachers is simple megalomania. I have never heard a single remark denoting any originality or vigour of mind. I have heard good, effective speaking in the side streets of Glasgow on a Saturday night. The speakers, however, were advocating not godliness but birth-control. Their object was to sell pamphlets about contraceptives, and they sold them.

The first call of outward-bound British steamers in Portugal is Leixoes (a name which nobody-can pronounce correctly, and few can spell), the seaport for Oporto. Oporto lies across the Douro, a few miles up the river; Leixoes, however, is not at the mouth of the Douro, but slightly to the north of it. British steamers, when they enter Leixs harbour at early morn, seem to make a point of waking the whole of Portugal with their sirens. Leixces, considered as a town, is nothing at all; it apparently has far more boats than houses. But we had no difficulty in hiring there a good car. In pursuance of the great principle that it is always wise to employ two men on a one-man job, this car was run by a couple of fellows, both very obliging and courteous. One of them did naught but wind up the car when necessary. The other was reported to be chauffeur to a Portuguese general; he was not in uniform, but this did not prevent us from being militarily saluted when we passed barracks. We had been warned about Portuguese roads and Portuguese driving, and the chauffeur-in-chief was earnestly exhorted to drive slowlyâ so that we could observe Portugal! Perhaps he did drive slowly, according to his conception of the adverb. But it is quite certain that he would go round absolutely blind corners in populous streets at thirty miles an hour. Nevertheless, no living thing was assassinated, and at the end of the day the car was still whole, though more loosely articulated than at the beginning. The roads were as appalling as rumour had made them, and the climate as exquisite.

The perils of the road were intensified by the numerous oxen-carts, which, to the exclusion of the horse, divide with the automobiles the road-traffic of the Oporto district. These carts must have started at the other end of civilisation some thousands of years ago, and they have now met the automobile at this end. Their massive wooden wheels have only two spokes. Their burden seems to be chiefly barrels. The pair of oxen, unshod, move at about two miles an hour, and take about a quarter of an hour to deflect themselves from the middle to the side of the street. A little boy walks between them, and a man sits behind and guides, without touching them, by means of a thing that looks like a goad, but is only a pointer. The Portuguese treat their animals in a reasonably sympathetic spirit. The yokes are works of applied art, elaborately carved, sometimes also painted in bright tints, and sometimes tufted as well. It is evident that they are handed down from generation to generation. The danger to automobiles of the oxen-carts lay in the far-spreading horns of the oxen. One lived throughout the day in the expectation of getting a horn-point in the eye. Whole families might have encamped under the shadow of those vast umbrageous horns.

The Douro is a beautiful river v ith precipitous, richly verdured banks, romantic, coquettish, and yet very dignified. And the little villages that border it, with their tiled fa9ades to prove that the Moors really existed, show a picturesqueness to match it. But the city of Oporto makes you forget the Douro. It is sublimely situated on various hills. From any summit its antique red roofs flow down in great curves to the dwarfed river, composing, amid the vivid greens and under the transparent blue, a picturesqueness that is merely marvellous. True, the greater and the lesser halves of Oporto are united by a very high iron bridge designed by the happily inimitable Eiffel, who ruined the entire aspect of Paris at one blow; but, unlike the Eiffel Tower, the Douro bridge is not everywhere visible. The winding and climbing configuration of Oporto is such that unless you are on a summit you can see only about ten yards of the city at once.

There is nothing of exciting interest in Oporto; the whole is more exciting and more lovely than any part. This is my own opinion, not the city's. The city is certainly capable of being excited by its Stock Exchange. And I admit that the Stock Exchange, though never achieving beauty, is imposing by reason of its dimensions, its costliness, its specially designed furniture, its floors, its granite staircases, its spittoons, its ballroom, and its general demonstration that the stockbrokers of Oporto, having determined to do something big, did it.

In the guardian of the Stock Exchange (not at the moment functioning) we had our first example of Portuguese expertness in throat-clearing, expectoration, and cigarette smoking. This man, like his race, had attractive manners and a mildly morose wit. When he led us into the Court of Commercial Justice, a great hall covered with bright frescoes, he said blandly: " Yes, but no justice in Portugal! Justice too high," and pointed to the figure of Justice portrayed on the lofty ceiling.

The Bourse was so exhausting that we had to go and have lunch, and, under advice, we went to the establishment entitled the Crystal Palace. It is on a summit, and so great that it has its own private railway-siding in its gardens. Within and without its ingenious ugliness is exacerbating â nearly, but not quite, as exacerbating as the ugliness of the original Crystal Palace. Still, we counted on the reputation of its cuisine. As the head waiter could speak a little French, I said to him, in reply to his request for the order: " We leave it to you. Give us the very best luncheon you can." He was flattered, as head waiters always are by this gambit. He gave us the very best luncheon he could. It comprised eight courses of solids, fine wines, fine cigars, fine liqueurs, and excellent coffee. And it was entirely admirable, with a touch of native originality. I doubt if you could get a better lunch outside Brussels, and we marvelled that a provincial town of moderate size could produce such a repast at ten minutes' notice. Clearly, the Portuguese understand eating, which is powerfully in their favour. The bill for three persons was monstrousâ fifteen thousand three hundred reis, less than thirty shillings. (Oh, rate of exchange!)

Thus fortified, we went to inspect the cathedral, which nobody seemed ever to have heard of. Apart from its cloisters, whose archaeological interest is considerable, the most interesting architectural thing about the cathedral is a dwelling-house which somebody negligently built, perhaps a century ago, high up between its towers. Exceedingly odd, this house! In front of the main entrance to the cathedral, at three o'clock in the afternoon, twenty or thirty lads and boys were playing and making an acute noise. They all helped us to find the residence of the sacristan, and most of them begged vociferously and were rewarded with British pennies. Some, however, did not beg. These got the first pennies. I asked one of them, who seemed rather mature, how old he was. " Eighteen." F 8i

Why this youth was not helping to do the world's work he did not explain.

The sacristan was cast in the same mould as the guardian of the Bourse. He showed us everything with great and bland deliberation. For him, the clou of the edifice was the bishops' robing-room, a splendid chamber, sombrely glittering with chased brass. Its main features were huge coffers full of ancient embroidered stuffs and a whole series of important mirrors. " What are all these mirrors for? " we demanded. The sacristan answered: " Bishops are just as human as other people. They like to look at themselves." We were silenced.

Feeling now that we had " done" Oporto, we joyfully realised that we were at liberty to search for second-hand shops and discover unprecedented bargains in the antique. We explored one street that was thick from end to end with jewellers offering rings at three million reis apiece; but nobody in the street had ever heard of a second-hand shop, and we came out of it having spent a mere ten thousand reis or so on Oporto silver-filigree work, which we assuredly should not have bought had not the rage for spending been upon us. We descended the high street of Oporto, and saw the rich bourgeoises of Oporto promenading with Latin and other dignity in black velvet. The assistant chauffeur sought to impress us with the information that the church tower at the top of the opposite slope was the highest in all the world! He also suggested that it would be a good plan to visit the pawnshops. We warmly welcomed the plan. We visited the pawnshops. What places! Up wide and rickety and filthy staircases with peeling walls, into dubious interiors (with pews for pawners) peopled by frowsy officials who bent over enormous and yellowed books of account. Balzacian places! But we drew blankâ absolutely blank. Then the assistant chauffeur delivered the news that his mother kept a secondhand shop. We flew to his mother, but the total value of her stock could not have exceeded two pounds.

At last, somehow, we had wind of a real second-hand shop. We drove there, impatient. The great door was locked. An employee reluctantly opened to our summons, and we had glimpses of long vistas of old furniture and bric-a-brac. We rejoiced. But the employee could do nothing for us. He said his master was away and that he himself knew not the price of things, and that, moreover, all the things "of an important value " were put away. He asked us, with kind nonchalance, to call again on Monday. (This was on a Friday.) But as we could not share his high and characteristic Portuguese contempt for time, we shook our heads and drove back in the beautiful, cold, clear evening to Leixs and the ship, where time was a tyrant.

Impossible to resist the conviction that the importance of Leixoes as a port was strangely-incommensurate with the importance of the city-it served. In the Douro we had noticed only one or two small steamers and schooners, and on its banks only one trifling shipyard. In Leixoss harbour were several large schooners, a Dutch steamer, a Japanese steamer, and a new American steamer (one of those which, according to an American present, take six weeks to build and six months to repair). Nothing else, save launches, smacks, and row-boats. No dock accommodation whatever. And this for a commercial city which is badly served by railways and through which passes all the port wine in the world. The last clause reminds me that I have said nothing of the famous " wine-lodges " of Oportoâ endless catacombs of port. We had purposely avoided them, frightened by the obligation to taste ten different ports in half an hour.

You go to the Portuguese Riviera from Lisbon by a special railway that runs along the north shore of the Tagus estuary, defacing it all the way, and ends at Cascaes. Cascaes stands at the beginning of the estuary, a fishing town to some extent residential, in whose apology for a harbour a pilot steamer lies night and day, for ever and ever, to catch arriving ships. Beyond Cascaes, civilisation ceases. The coast-line curves round to the north, and for a great distance there is nothing but lighthouses, dunes, ceaseless and immense breakers, and bold capes. The authorities have constructed a good road from Cascaes north, but, after proceeding courageously for several miles, it finishes in sand. One heard of a project for a pleasure-town somewhere in those fine wastes, and one will probably continue to hear of the project for many years to come. If ever the thing is conjured into existence the inhabitants will live in an eternal booming of breakers, comparable to that of Treasure Island.

Between Lisbon and Cascaes the shore is a necklace of townlets strung on to the railway line. They touch one another, so that in a duration of an hour and a distance of less than twenty miles the train stops about twenty times. At some points the time between starting from one station and starting from the next scarcely exceeds a minute, and the hotel porters do not hurry in fixing your baggage; if the train moves off while they are on board, they just let it take them to the next station and then gently walk backâ an affair of five minutes. The trains are by no means trains de luxe, or expresses, but they do exhibit the chief virtue of a trainâ they are prompt. The line is no doubt one of the most efficient in

Portugal. And the roads, speaking generally, were the best we saw in Portugal. In fact, it was plain that the district must be inhabited hy people of influence who knew how to look after the amenities of their life. A number of the residents were " daily-breaders," commutersâ otherwise season-ticket holders. They behaved, however, in a Portuguese fashion. You could see them walking calmly to the station as the train was arriving. Not a sign of haste. The train would stop in the station. Still not a sign of hurry. Then the train would whistle and puff, and then only would the commuters run. Of course they missed the train; but there would be another in three-quarters of an hour, and the day had twenty-four hours. Impossible to deny that these commuters understood the value of possessing their souls in philosophic tranquillity.

As the line gets farther from Lisbon so does the character of the townlets develop until, in the Estoril region, which consists of three contiguous townletsâ St. John Estoril, Estoril, and Mont Estorilâ the architecture becomes fantastic, orchidaceous, incredible. There are hundreds, thousands, of villas, at different elevations on the slopes, and each is more marvellous than the others. Architectural tradition is simply ignored in the majority of these gleaming white, pink, blue, and yellow houses. They caricature mediseval castles, Italian renaissance palaces, English country-houses. They are frescoed; they are fretted; they are inlaid. Some are rather good; a few grotesquely miss fire, but none is ordinary. Seen in the mass, during a soft, lucid sunset, they come nearer to constituting a fairyland than anything else modern I ever saw. The most extravagant of all the confections, a building that again and again we would walk a mile and a half to see, proved to be a garage. Far more grandiose than the house to which it was attached, it resembled nothing in the history of evolution. It was superbly ugly, but it exercised a most potent spell. We inquired about it from a lady who had resided long in the district. " Yes," she said, " that was built by a man who felt sorry for an architect who could never get anything to do." I doubt not that it was the only job that the architect ever got. But he has not lived in vain.

The Estoril region is the tripartite queen of the Portuguese Riviera. It lies next to Cascaes, and is on the part of the northern shore which juts out beyond the southern shore of the estuary, so that the view therefrom is of the unbounded sea. It appears to consist exclusively of villas, hotels, and little casinos. The absence of chimneys strikes an Englishman, but the climate explains that. Less explicable is the dearth of shops. Shops there were, but very few and very paltry.

And by what machinery of distribution physical life was sustained in the region we never discovered. Mont Estoril is supposed to dominate the three Estorils; it is easily the best known of the three in the great Anglo-Saxon community of globetrotters. But its days of domination appear to be numbered. Estoril (between Mont and St. John) is erecting a tremendous pleasure park on a quite cosmopolitan scale, and comprising hotels, baths, a casino, and even arcades of shops. When this dream is fulfilledâ and it is very nearly fulfilled, for the glass is in most of the million windowsâ Mont will have to take second place, and will then, of course, make a point of its select quietude. The new hotels are not likely to be better, in essentials, than the plain but well-run and moderately priced hotels of Mont Estoril, which in the methods of their excellent management seem to be Swiss or Italian.

But all these things are nothing. The chief matter in the Portuguese Riviera is the climate. We spent February there. On the first morning I went out before breakfast under the bluest sky and the most magnificent sunshine I have experienced anywhere save in the Sahara. I did not put on an overcoat; it would have been monstrous to put on an overcoat. Well, the east wind went through me like a dagger through a ghost. Never have I met with an east wind so dead east as that wind. Half an hour of it gave me neuralgia for three days. But ere the three days had elapsed the climate had relented, and it soon grew to be paradisaical. In a week we loved it, and girls were bathing in the sea. (True, they were Scottish girls.) The climate is vastly superior to that of the French Rivieraâ you can be frozen to death on one side of the Avenue de la Republique at Nice and roasted to death on the otherâ if only for the fact that the temperature scarcely falls at night. Indeed, the nights are warm in winter. Clemency is the true name of the climate. We had three days of rain, and at the end of our stay somebody broke it to us that February was the rainy month. Undoubtedly the most favoured periods would be the six weeks beginning the 1st of Marchâ when the wild flowers, of which we saw the infancy, must cover the hill-slopes with colourâ and the six weeks beginning the ist of October. In summer, it appears, great winds blow, and the shores are crammed and bursting with Portuguese parents and babies. (After all, it is their country.) -Â Cintra is one of the show places of Portugal. It used to beâ in Southey's time, for instance â one of the show places of the world. You reach it from the Estorils northward across a rising, rolling, austere country of scrubby trees and umber earth which is enlivened by bright gorse, a huge decaying palace or so, a penal agricultural settlement, and a few unkempt, picturesque villages whose inhabitants are very-much patched and not in the slightest degree picturesque. The villages, however, are perhaps not as barbaric as they appear, for a tumbledown house in one of the most remote of them bore an inscription in Portuguese signifying, "United Recreative Club of Pinho."

Having turned the flank of a sierra, you perceive Cintra lying on the northern slope thereof, high above a vast plain lined with obviously good roads that lead to the glittering Atlantic. The horses have never stopped trotting. They will unremittingly trot eight, ten, twelve miles, gently but steadily, accepting ceaseless hills with calm fatalism; they continue, they continue. Occasionally the driver reminds them of the seriousness of their vocation with a flick; he does not lash, or even whip.

The whole of the district, including Cintra, is dominated by the palace of Pena, set on a peak in the clouds. The Moors probably had good reason to build there. The Prince Consort, who tried to improve on them by grandiosely imitating media? valism in the middle of the nineteenth century, had no good reason. Only a vain and lunatic fool would have imposed on the labour of his country the heartrending task of transporting to the summit of the sierra the materials for this incredible mass of architectural mediocrity.

Such fantastic tricks must put a strain on the great principle of divine right.

Cintra itself is dominated by a twin pair of bottle-like or kiln-like or gourd-like constructions that spring with a curious abnormality from the roofs of the royal palace in the centre of the town. You want to investigate those twins, and you want still more to have lunch; but you are a tourist and therefore the slave of tradition, and the unchangeable tradition is that before lunch tourists must persist for several miles beyond the town in order to visit the gardens of Monserrate, once the home of Beckford of Fonthill and Vathek â double-asterisked in the pre-war Baedeker. You know in advance that the gardens of Monserrate will be a bore. They are. True, they are less of a bore than the gigantic, world-renowned private gardens of Bordighera, but simply because they are less extensive. The detested landscape gardener has created them the negation of a garden; and all the captive trees are rare, and every tree has' a label in clear Latin tied round its neck. There are two redeeming merciesâ no guide is permitted to accompany you, and the gardeners are not labelled.

The delayed lunch at the Hotel Netto atones. You see at once that the head waiter, in a white jacket, is a human being. He is urbane, grave, dignified. He does not ask you what you will have for lunch. He brings you the lunchâ and promptlyâ receiving it himself, course by course, through an aperture like a ticket-window at a railway station. It is an excellent lunch, from the omelette, of which you have heard the sizzling on the other side of the aperture, to the oranges on their stalks. The waiter knows it is an excellent lunch. About the Collares wine he allows himself a discreet enthusiasm, for it is a special vintage of the hotel. He is a careful man. He will not serve your drivers until he has bowed down to your ear like a butler and ascertained that you intend them to lunch at your expense. You feel that he comprehends human nature. He has character and he can weigh the character in you, and he takes a tip with neither servility nor condescension. There is again character in the middle-aged women outside who cajole money out of your pocket in exchange for adequate sweetmeats and quite inadequate post cards. They, too, are urbane and dignified, and yet with a dash of flirtatious or roguish insistence. Poverty has not caused them to forget that they were once girls and are still very feminine. They win, and you accept defeat with relish.

But the most human human beings in the town are certainly the custodians of the summer palace. The first greets you from his cubicle at the top of the first flight of steps. Having taken your money, he emerges to welcome you, not as an official, but as a fellow-man. You perceive unmistakably that he is enormous; that he is rubicund, that he is juicy, that the savour of life distends his great nostrils. He smiles richly. He is like a man of butter in a blue suit. It might be said of him that his paths drop fatness. He gives you the illusion that nobody has ever visited the palace before, and that your advent is a milestone in his career, and that if all the moments could be like that moment he would scorn to receive wages for guarding the palace. He abounds on every side of you for ten paces, and then suddenly, in broken French, informs you that it is forbidden to him to accompany you farther. At his suggestion you ascend another flight of steps and ring a bell. You do ring. No answer. The custodian below grins and makes a furious motion of the arm to indicate that you aren't half ringing. You ring with sternness. He approves. The door is opened by Custodian Number Two, while Number One beams upward, as if saying, "Precisely what I said would come to pass has come to pass."

Number Two is thinner â an India-paper encyclopaedia of the palace. Though not servile, he is a courtier, and, though a courtier, he is very firm. He may be distinguished from all other officials in Portugal by the fact that he is not smoking a cigarette and does not spitâ even into a spittoon. The excellent adroit fellow has really nothing to show, but he shows it with grandeur. Except Moorish tiles and a few suits of armour and the chimneys of the tremendous Moorish kitchen (which are in truth the bottlelike constructions dominating the town), there is naught of the slightest aesthetic or practical interest in the whole castle. No worse pictures were ever painted than hang on these walls.

There are, however, the private apartments. " Please abandon your cigarette," says Number Two. " I am about to show you the private apartments of the ex-king and queen." A proof, this, of the existence of the historic sense in a republican official. Poor, dark little private apartments! You see how monarchs till quite recently lived in their summer villegiatura, and the revelation is pathetic. The chief of the furniture is protected from you by a cord, in imitation of Fontainebleau. What furniture! What a tasteless, vulgar mixture of styles and no-styles! The desk of the assassinated Carlos might have been bought at a celebrated second-, hand establishment in Kingsway, The leather arm-chair might have come out of a hotel, the plush sofa out of a dubious house. It is terrible, desolating, frightful. It would not be believed on the stageâ no, not on the provincial stage. The bedroom, after the other rooms, is comparatively innocuous. The washstand shows modern plumbing, coquettishly finished. Here the queen used to bend with pride over a hot-water tap device invented in Englandâ the same queen who, with a bouquet of flowers her sole weapon, tried to shield her husband from the bullets of a political executioner in Lisbon.

When you get out of the palace the unctuous and jolly Number One runs forth rapidly at you, as you pass, with buttonhole posies. A delicate attention! You must accept them or break his heart. Remunerate him or not as you chooseâ that is a detailâ but accept the offering of a brother.

After the palace, nothing in Cintra! An agreeable enough little town, with a real train and two or three tram-cars, and a bookshop (where tobacco maintains the balance of the balance-sheet), but scarcely worthy to be the cynosure of a continent. Byron wrote bits of Childe Harold there. You can see the building; it was and is a hotel. The mimosa is perfectly marvellousâ mimosa in full blossom meets mimosa across the thoroughfares in winter. No doubt in summer the display of vegetation is prodigious. And what then? As a resort, as a public monument, Cintra must decay. The modern tourist is more aware of relative values than Southey was, or Byron, who compared the town to Eden. The globe is more familiar to him.

A word concerning Pena. Geographically it is only about half a mile from Cintra, but as it is on a crag just a third of a mile high, the hairpin road from town to Pena is probably several miles in length; even so, its gradients are such as effectively to cure the magnificent horses of their habit of trotting. As you ascend, the scenery takes on a more and more panoramic grandeur, and Cintra gets smaller and smaller, and before you are anywhere near the gates of the park you can look down the champagne-bottle chimneys of the summer palace in the middle of the town. The feature of the luxuriant mountain-side is the immense boulders, some of them weighing a hundred tons or so, poised on one another like the transient edifice of a child. The Lisbon earthquake must have put the fear of Heaven into those boulders for a few years. The hanging gardens out of which the towers of Pena rise are full of black swans and fountains, and the February climate may be judged from the fallen camellia blossom that lies everywhere.

The great castle is surrounded by a narrow terrace, and the tremendous views from this terrace are in the highest degree sublime. Nothing finer can exist outside Yellowstone Park. If Southey lived on the peak before the Arabian remains were rendered habitable, then he is justified of his words. Byron is not. The affair is overwhelming, but it bears no resemblance to the Edens of the old illustrated family Bibles. Possibly Eden may be located in the Moorish castle whichâ though from the town it seems almost as lofty as Penaâ is now perched far below on a lesser crag. When you enter the modern residence, all is over, for you are in one of the worst royal houses ever seen. True, there are a very few fine things, and especially there is an Italian fifteenth-century alabaster altar (which must have needed some engineering up these slopes); but the ensemble is uglier even than the interior of the palace in the town. The inconveniences, the discomforts, the pettinesses, the obscurities, the monstrosities are simply tragic. Only one room. Queen Amelia's chamber, had a fireplaceâ seemingly transported from Cromwell Road. Look on the wall at the Christmas card (with an English greeting) hand-painted by King Carlos, and at the water-colours by the same and by Queen Amelia. Look at the yellowing periodical literature (all dated October 19lo) scattered aboutâ Modern Society (" the mirror of the social world "), Gil Bias â and the Gazette des Beaux-Arts. Look at the cheaply framed reproductions of old masters, issued at a shilling apiece by William Heinemann. Search in vain for the bathroom. But every little window frames a celestial view. The Prince Consort climbed seventeen hundred feet to erect all this formidable masonry into the false semblance of something antique and fine; he employed a colonel as architect; he spent a fortune to produce G an abode that any stockbroker would sniff at; he desecrated a unique, miraculous site, and in sixty years of use a royal line failed to make the place better than a congeries of expensive wigwams. The last sound and the first which we heard within the castle was that of an oil-engine. Doubtless it was employed to actuate the dynamo for the " wireless " installation whose wires are now stretched between the towers of the great eyesore. The republic has had the wit to turn to utility a monument which ought not to exist, but which it would be foolish to destroy.

One of the most satisfactory things about Lisbon is that you can enter it from the sea without any passport formalities. Indeed at no Portuguese port had we to show passports or to give any information whatever as to our foreign selves. We might have been emissaries of Lenin carrying the seeds of conspiracy and Bolshevism, for all the Portuguese authorities seemed to care. Travellers in Europe will admit that this is a great point in favour of Portugal.

As for the renowned view of Lisbon from the river, I have seen finer views of cities from the water. It was good but did not induce ecstasy. The view from the highest of the hundred hills upon which Lisbon is built was much more striking than the view from the river.

The city has importance, but exactly how important it is nobody knows. In 1900 it had a population of three hundred and fifty thousand. Just before the war it was supposed to have a population of half a million or more. To-day, such has been the influx from the countryside, the lowest estimate puts the population at three-quarters of a million, and some statisticians with a love of round figures put it at a million. But only the next census will discover the truth. Anyhow, the city has a frontage of seven miles to the Tagus, which is somethingâ especially along the Lisbonian streets. The pity is that the most glorious sight in Lisbonâ the church and monastery of Belem (the latter now a well-run orphanage)â lies at the wrong end of the seven miles. The spectacularly remarkable thing about Lisbon is the fact that, owing to the number and precipitateness of its hills (some of them rise at an angle within a few degrees of the perpendicular), half the buildings appear to be perched on top of the other half. The crest of one hill is reached by an elevator that ends in a short horizontal gallery. To erect this elevator right in the middle of the city was a stroke of genius on the part of the city council. Of course the elevator itself is ugly, but it is well masked by big buildings, and the panorama from the summit at dusk is of a magical beauty. The time to see the romance of Lisbon is after the glare of the sun on the white, pink, and yellow buildings has begun to fade, when the washed clothes that flow down on poles from the windows of every storey in the quieter streets have lost their intimate detail in the twilight and become mysterious. And even the most modern white streets of the shopping centre look lovely at night in the diffused radiance of arc-lamps often hidden round a corner; they are monumental then, simplified, grandiose, immensely impressive. And " Oriental" Lisbon, ravines of streets, climbing, descending, curving, is as picturesque as anyone can desire.

The population everywhere intensifies the picturesqueness, for it is thoroughly mixed, diversified, and tinted in all shades. Every variety of cross from 99 per cent. Latin-Moorish and I per cent, negro, to 99 per cent, negro and I per cent. Latin-Moorish, can be seen; and racial purity of any sort is rare. There is no colour prejudice in Portugal; there could not be. You can see the races of the earth in Chicago, if you visit different quarters, but in Lisbon you can see the races of the earth in a single individual. This complexity of breeding appears especially strange in the central square of Lisbon, where newspaper-offices, hotels, restaurants, cafes, stores, picture-theatres, gaming-houses, and a spider's web of electric tram-wires give a physical illusion of unadulterated Western modernity.

Lisbon is as different from Oporto as New
York from, say, New Orleans. Not less picturesque, but differently picturesque. One meets few oxen in Lisbon, and the Lisbon oxen have plain yokes and horns less like the antlers of a stag. On the other hand, there is a full and even generous supply of automobiles, and the picturesqueness of these is vocal; it consists in the noise they make and the wind of their rushing. A story runs that a Portuguese profiteer bought a Rolls-Royce, and the next day complained that it was not satisfactory. The vendor anxiously interviewed the chauffeur, who said that the car functioned to perfection. But the owner protested:

"Nothing of the kind. It's absolutely noiseless. You can't hear it move."

The vendor soon remedied that defect and made the owner quite happy. When you are trying to sleep, and not succeeding, at the Avenida Palace Hotel, which gives on the famous Avenue of Liberty (a respectable but dull imitation of the Champs Elysees), the row, din, and uproar of the automobiles of Portuguese profiteers develop into a phenomenon surpassing all other phenomena on earthâ and it is a phenomenon that persists during twenty-one hours of the twenty-four. Compared to it. Fifth Avenue is like a side-street in Concord, and Piccadilly like a churchyard. Possibly cross-breeding may account for this excruciating passion for noise and restlessness which to my mind removes Lisbon from quite the van of the procession of progress.

Nevertheless, Lisbon is in the movement. Its picture-theatres are packed, and Charlie Chaplin and Mary Pickford are adored there. Its huge opera-house, with a hundred private boxes and a shoe-shine parlour, attracts considerable audi- ences to performances that compare not unfavourably with those of Paris. It has libraries. It has national art collections (though the rules for admittance thereto tend to dissuade the visitor from attempting to see them). It has fire-engines, which fly toward con-flagrations to a warning accompaniment of tin whistles. It has lots of newspapers; it has a theatrical newspaper. It has one or two good restaurants, and one very good indeedâ but not better than at Oporto. It has strikes. It has many strikes. I should not be surprised to learn that Portugal has more strikes per square mile and per head than any other country in the world. In Oporto the trams had struck. No sooner had we entered the restaurant of our first hotel in Lisbon than we had to assist at a strike in the making. The proceedings were conducted in French. With a magnificent disregard of hungry clients, the waiters crowded round the hated employer, who demanded of them with all the arts of rhetoric: " Am I the master here or are you? " If I had been asked to reply, I should have said: " Neither of you. And that's either the curse or the salvation of the situationâ I don't know which." Still, the affair tranquillised itself, and we obtained our mealâ not a good one. The telephones in Lisbon had been on strike for weeks and weeks. The postal service was so disorganised that enterprising firms would organise their own service when they could. The railways were on the eve of striking. But the Portuguese have the art of life, which is the attainment of calm and of fatalism.

You could see the art of life in full practice in the sugar-queues, which abounded in the streets as sugar itself abounded in the hotels; you noticed respectably dressed old gentlemen standing placidly in these queues, and still standing there when you passed the same spot two hours later. You could see it in the use of the monocles which the golden youth and middle-age of Portugal deem to be an essential part of their raiment. An official told us that ten thousand monocles of plain glass were imported into Lisbon every year. The same official told us that forty thousand persons were employed in the gambling trade in Portugal; that there were four hundred gambling-houses in Lisbon, and over a hundred within a hundred yards of the Rocioâ the central square of the city; and he told us further that since business men had a habit of gambling till 2 or 3 a. m., it was difficult to make appointments with them before noon.

We gradually came under the obsession of the great Portuguese gambling idea. We heard again and again that the best food at the cheapest prices and the best dancing and the best diversions generally were to be had in the gambling-houses of Lisbon. And at length we determined to visit the most chicâ of course solely in the interests of social science! We arranged a rendezvous for nine o'clock, because our information was that nobody would dream of dining in a Lisbon gambling-house before nine-thirty. As the hour approached we grew positively excited, and we drove up to the door in a fever of anticipation. The door was shut. A small crowd of young quidnuncs said that the place was closed by order. Impossible! Everybody had agreed that the authorities would never dare to shut up the gambling-houses. We tried another one. Closed! Another. Closed! Lastly we went, under guidance, to a mysterious establishment in a dark and dubious street. Our guide said that the authorities would not succeed in closing that. Closed! Presently we became aware of cavalrymen prancing up and down the thoroughfares in couples. The thing looked like a revolution. But it was only the Portuguese method of closing gambling-houses. The next morning a military sentry stood in front of the door of each of the four hundred gambhng-houses at Lisbon. Naturally we rejoiced, as virtuous and hard-working men, at the suppression of this terrible vice. Yes, we rejoiced. But somewhere in the recesses of our minds was a notion to the effect that the Portuguese Government would have done well to postpone the suppression for just twenty-four hours. We had to leave Portugal without the slightest notion of what kind of a paradise a truly chic Lisbon gambling-house really is. A few days later the English papers talked descriptively of a revolution in Portugal. But we knew what it was and that it wasn't a revolution.

From British inhabitants and frequenters of Portugal we heard various verdicts on the Portuguese. One man said that Portugal was corrupt from top to bottomâ from the policeman on the pier to the chief of the state; that the profiteers had taken all the best houses, that the house famine was extremely acute, that no effort whatever was being made to cure it, and, finally, that the middle classes were being ground to powder between the millstone of the profiteer and the millstone of the proletariat. Nothing in this indictment struck us as novel. We had heard much the same of other countries that could eat Portugal without too much indigestion. The general verdict was decidedly more favourable. Foreigners who had spent their lives in

Portugal spoke well of the Portuguese. They said that the were polite, amenable, and satisfactory to deal with, provided that you could smile pleasantly and refrain from trying to hustle them. To try to hustle them was fatal. They held strongly that Portugal was deserving of the utmost possible sympathetic treatment, seeing that it had gone into the war with expectation of great advantage, and come out of the war with nothing but high prices and debt. And they attributed the relative instability of government not to the capriciousness of the people, but to the absence of permanent officials in the state-machine. Strange to say, terrible to relate, the Portuguese people, unlike more imposing races, are not faultless. Nevertheless we, in our brief acquaintance, took a considerable fancy to them.

On the Wednesday before the threatened railway strike I took stock of Hyde Park. Kensington Gardens, barred to the pubhc, was a white-tented field. G. S. waggons moved to and fro in it, and soldiers, either in groups or singly, walked about with an earnest but quite unsuccessful pretence of executing a great war. A non-commissioned officer caressed his thigh by means of a cane. The big refreshment-kiosk, with waitresses in white aprons all complete, was openâ possibly for the convenience of the Great General Staff. I heard continuously the distant menacing roll of a drum. Close by me was a newly-erected wireless station, no doubt getting hourly news of the flooding of mines by Scottish miners and their attacks on volunteer pump-workers.

In the Row were many scores of horsemen and horsewomenâ whole families of them, dwindling down from immense papa to the budding flapper on a Shetland. Men were tightening the girths of women's mounts with the most chivalrous attention. And the Row was flanked by processions of nun-like nursemaids pushing single prams and double pramsâ the Rolls-Royces of the pram-world, magnificently hooded to protect august infants.

I wandered towards Knightsbridge Barracks, and had the greatest luck. A full military band filed out into the yard, and was followed by an old military officer, wondrously shaved, mous-tached, clothed, legginged, booted, and spurred. (His valet or batman must have led a full life.) This military officer amounted to the mirror, symbol, paragon, and exemplar of utter correctness. He seemed quite ready to conduct battles on an immense scale, but he strangely carried in his gloved hands a baton, and instead of a battle he conducted that very fine fox-trot, "Avalon." Though his gestures were nonchalant enough, and he experienced none of Sir Henry Wood's difficulty in keeping hair out of eyes, the performance of " Avalon " was admirable. It uplifted the heart, unbent the mind, tranquillised the soul, and put a better complexion on the Empire.

Nobody among the small group of nursemaids, quidnuncs, and me applauded the fox-trot. Nevertheless the military officer repeated the performance, and I was glad. At the end of the second performance he gave a third. And then a fourth. My mettle was aroused. I said to myself: " I can stand him as long as he can conduct ' Avalon." " I was mistaken. He beat me. When at last I retreated, he was still nonchalantly conducting glorious performances of " Avalon.". The insistent throbbing of the distant drum regained my ear.

The new generationâ I mean the generation which in 1914 was just old enough to fight, nurse, or otherwise serve in the Warâ probably shows a more striking change from the one before it than any generation has shown for at least two centuries. A change in mind, spirit, and manner! The change of manner, of course, irritates a large number of persons who are shocked because the world continues to go round after they have begun to suffer from rheumatism and baldness. The changes of mind and spirit, however, are more important. As regards mind, the latest generation is better educated, more cultivated, less hypocritical, more courageous, more honest, less stuffy than its predecessors, and in all these respects has quite marvellously improved on its predecessor's predecessors. Further, it has completed a sort of revolution in the relations of the sexes, which aforetime were regulated by a system of conventions, shams, and pretences that can only be described as poisonous.

As regards the spirit, the latest generation has rediscovered, or is rediscovering, the great secrets â lost since the Elizabethan Ageâ that the chief thing in life is to feel that you are fully alive, that continual repression is absurd, that dullness is a social crime, that the present is quite as important as the future, that life oughtn't to be a straight line but a series of ups and downs, and that moments of ecstasy are the finest moments and the summits of existence. It has finally killed the Victorian Age dead. I am willing to admit that the Victorian Age was a great age, though it acutely exasperated me when I was young. But that it had the terrible vices of continual repression and disgusting hypocrisy cannot be disputed, and to contemplate its corpse gives me genuine pleasure. So much for the achievement of the latest generation. The latest generation hasn't done everything itself, but it has handsomely finished what others began, and it shall be awarded the glory. Personally, I rejoice even in its mistakes.

Now the most spectacular symptom of the new spirit is the revival and the full democratisa-tion of dancing. The latest generation certainly did not initiate the revival, which began long before the War in the formation of private dance clubs, whose fault was a ridiculous snobbishness. What the latest generation did was to seize on to a good thing, to exploit it fully, and to tear it free of the chains of convention and expose it to all the antiseptic winds of publicity.

It is to the demands of the latest generation that we owe the public dance-halls which are among the most impressive, beautiful, and healthy phenomena of modern social life. Not that the

dance-halls are the recent invention of the middle class in London and the great provincial centres, as some might assume. Dance-halls flourished mightily even in the last century in a few of the most popular seaside resorts, especially at Blackpool and at Douglas, Isle of Man. In these considerable pleasure cities there were dance-halls before the latest generation was born, and before the fox-trot and the shimmy had been conceived. The halls were efficiently managed, with few but rigidly enforced rules; they had good music; they were bright and even glittering; and they were cheap. (You had the run of them for sixpence a head.) They did, as they still do, enormous business, and were largely responsible for the popularity of the two places named. Years and years ago I used to watch them functioning with amazement and delight, and I wondered that they did not attract attention from students of social phenomena. True, in those days students of social phenomena had not yet removed the blinkers prepared for them by Ruskin, Mill, Carlyle, and Lord Shaftesbury.

But the halls were naturally closed for the greater part of the year, appealing exclusively to holiday-makers in definite seasons of holiday, which depended on weather conditions and on the caprices of railway companies. It never occurred to me, and I doubt if it occurred to anyone, that plain people might care to dance publicly in the evenings of working-days, or that sea air was not absolutely essential to dancing, or that it was not necessary to travel a hundred miles in order to enjoy a dance, or that the desire to dance, like the desire to eat, drink, and love, might possibly be quite independent of all seasons whatever. These great discoveries came later, and they did not come through the dance-halls of the industrial classes, which dance-halls were regarded by the other classes as amusingly vulgar. The industrial class had indeed started public dancing on a scale undreamed of by Cremorne and Ranelagh, and with vastly more decorum; but the industrial class only found out that dancing might be just as delectable in winter as in summer through its habit of imitating the classes above it. The dancing " craze," as the lame and halt and senile describe it, percolated both downwards and upwards from the middle class through the strata of society, and to-day there is no class which does not dance, and probably no class which objects to be seen dancing in public or in semi-public. That which once was amusingly vulgar is now strictly correctâ and still amusing.

Halls, clubs, and subscription organisations exist everywhere in order that individuals may dance amid a crowd consisting mainly of individuals personally unknown to them. The entertainment is one at which every spectator is also a performerâ and not merely a performer, but an ecstatic, thrilled, and joyous performer. The resulting spectacle is unique, in addition to being grand. It is inspiring. It means the public and the frank re-establishment of joy and ecstasy. And, incidentally, it shows how indestructible are the most ancient human instincts. The dance is probably older than anything except eating, drinking, love, and murder.

The curious and convenient thing is that dancing provides joy and ecstasy and the uplifting of the soul, and at the same time does positive moral, artistic, and physical good to the dancer. It has practically none of the disadvantages which accompany other forms of diversion and exercise and discipline. You can get ecstasy out of a bottle of champagne or even a glass of beer (not to speak of six glasses), but the uplifting is no finer than what the dance affords; it is, in fact, less fine, and it has grave drawbacks, some of which may not be noticed for years, and some of which are very apt to be noticed the next morning. And dancing is a physical exercise quite as efficacious as, and far less tedious than, the ingenious contortions prescribed by training experts. Its effect upon the action of the skin is excellent; it develops the muscles; it renders the body lissom; and it fosters gracefulness of carriage. Further, it cannot fail to teach rhythm â an important matter which most citizens would remain quite ignorant of if they did not dance. The mere discipline of moving accurately to music is valuable; and so is the discipline of co-ordinating one's movements with the movements of another person.

In nearly all these respects modern dancing is probably superior to the dancing of earlier centuries, which was much slower and which certainly was not calculated to induce ecstasy. Modern dancing would have shocked the eighteenth century, and yet the eighteenth century was more cynical and less moral than the twentieth.

Finally, in the catalogue of dancing's merits, there is the fact that, unlike golf and other crudities, it is practised when people are in their best and prettiest clothes and on their best behaviour. To sum up, I would say that the " craze" for dancing is a truly healthy and hopeful sign of these times which are so rich in signs doubtful and sinister.

I shall not let my enthusiasm carry me into the clouds. Willingly will I be the stern moralist and adopt the grave tone so much admired in this country. I assert solemnly that public dancing has its evil side. (No! Not the evil side which is perhaps in your minds, and the existence of which I do not for a moment credit!)

It keeps its devotees up too late. The law ordains a certain hour for closing public resorts and clubs, but the law makes frequent exceptions, and, moreover, there are well-known devices for evading the law. I am not an advocate of early-dancing; I have no use for afternoon dancing, and assuredly I do not believe in dancing between the courses at dinner. But I think that people ought to know when to go home, and that too many of them, even if they do know, lack the moral fibre to act on their knowledge. Dancers who go home at 3 a. m. must cheat either themselves or somebody else the next day; for there are not and never will be twenty-seven hours in a day. The disadvantage is real; it is serious; and every effort should be made to minimise it.

In regard to the actual art of dancing as exemplified to-day in public and semi-public ballrooms, it may be said to be full of interesting problems, the solution of one or two of which may one day catastrophically split the dancing world into two camps. Perhaps for many people, especially people with plenty of money in their pockets, the really acute problem, quite unconnected with the art of dancing, is where to find a hall or club that on the one hand is not so fashionably packed that you can't move, or on the other hand is not so unfashionably and forlornly empty that you feel in it as if you were assisting at a memorial service for the death of dancing.

A great problem, of a moral or political nature, now just simmering up, is raised by the question: " Why should the man always absolutely rule the dance? " There is no answer to this question except to say that women have ever been in subjection and therefore should ever be. In any dance of a couple one of the pair must of course be autocrat, but why should not the pair exchange roles at intervals? Women know as much about dancing as men, and numbers of them could certainly direct the mutual movements better than the men with whom they dance. I am surprised that our more advanced feminists out of a job have not made a fuss over such a fundamental affair long since.

But the problem of problems is the admitted monotony of modern dancing. A few weeks ago I beheld with amazement the programme of a ball at Buckingham Palace. With the exception of the formal opening grand quadrille and the final galop, every dance was a waltz. There were about twenty waltzes one after the other. Not a fox-trot! As for a one-step!. As for a tango!. It may have been held, and perhaps wisely, that words such as " fox-trot" would not look nice on the pasteboards of a Buckingham Palace ball. But even in other ballrooms the programmes are monotonous.

The one-step has fallen into disfavour, and rightly so, for it is a tenth-rate business. Programmes are divided in the main between foxtrots and waltzes, and though the waltz is a finer dance than the fox-trot, the fox-trot is still very fine, and, being easier than the waltz and better adapted for variations, it immensely exceeds the waltz in popularity. The mischief is that the steps of the two dances are identical. Again, the authorities who govern and judge competitions will not permit any sort of stunt effectsâ and who shall blame them? So that there is in practice almost no lawful outlet for the human yearning after change and variety.

Serious efforts are being made to popularise the tango in London. There is only one waltz, but there are seventy-and-seven tangos, and the tango is a great dance, with the magnificent rhythm of the fox-trot but slower; and if you know enough you might dance tangos for a whole evening and scarcely repeat your figures. But I do not see much future for the genuine tango in Great Britain. The tango is growing old. It has been the rage of Paris, where every second dance was and is a tango; but what has been the rage of Paris is not destined to long life in the rest of the world. In London to this day, when a tango is played, the majority of the dancers keep timidly off the floor and watch the dancing minority. This is a cautious island.

Nor do I think that any form of the square or the round dance will return in our time. Though the custom of one couple sticking together for a whole season may slowly disappear â and I hope it will, for it has a malign influence upon the woman's dancing and renders the male dancer even more self-centred than he otherwise would beâ dancing must remain an intimacy of two in public. Dancing cannot be really popular unless it is public, for not one person in a hundred thousand possesses a ballroom, and square or round dances are impossible at a public dance. What is more, they are not so interesting to the performers as the couple-dance. The great need of the age is a new step, with new figures, capable of many variations within a few clear rules. Such a novelty, combined with the fox-trot and the waltz, would remove the reproach of monotony.

In France an accused person is assumed to be guilty till he has proved himself innocent, but we boast that in Britain he is presumed to be innocent till he is proved guilty.

The boast is fairly justified as regards the bench, but I doubt if it is fairly justified as regards the police and the prison authorities. The mere phrase "In the dock" has a sinister sound, implying guilt before guilt is proved. In most courts the dock is so designed and arranged as to make its occupant seem like a criminal. Yet throughout every trial every accused person, until the verdict is pronounced, is presumed to be an innocent man. Why, then, seek to make him look guilty?

The other day a prisoner could not be put into the dock because there was no dock ready for him. The moral effect of his not being in the dock was quite startling. The dock ought to be conceived in a different spirit, a spirit which remembers that the occupants are legally innocent.

It may happen to any innocent personâ it has happened to tens of thousands of innocent personsâ to get into the hands of the police late at night, for the police are human, like the rest of us, and err. The prisoner is for the time being legally innocent. Is he treated as innocent?

Not a bit. He is pushed into a cell which is generally very dirty, and always excessively uncomfortable, and always without elementary conveniences; and if he is to sleep he must sleep on wood. This is the preparation given to him for fighting the whole force of the law next day. The cells at police stations are at this hour an outrageous scandal. They might at least be kept clean, even if it costs money to keep them clean; and there ought to exist devices for making them comfortable. Why should an innocent person be compelled to pass a night on a plank in conflict with filth, fleas, and bugs?

The worst thing of all is the astounding reluctance of magistrates to give reasonable bail, and especially to give bail on the prisoner's own recognisances. If bail is not granted, a legally innocent man goes to prison. You understand: prison. He has certain minor privileges, the chief of which he must pay forâ if he can, but he is a prisoner, a captive, a shamed captive, a soul cut off suddenly from the whole world. Magistrates ought always to give bail unless to do so would be patently ridiculous. Not long ago a woman was brought to trial who had been imprisoned for seven weeks. The law presumed her innocent, but the police, under order of a magistrate, had kept her in confinement for over fifty days. Imagine the dreadful effect on her mind and on her body. The judge described her offence as " comparatively trivial " and gave her a nominal sentence of three days. The judge said she had been imprisoned " through some stupendous blunder." But will she receive compensation? She will not.

A great deal of our legal system is totally barbaric. It is not merely unjust. It is infamous.

Â NTARio

Once I inspected a huge prison, under the guidance of the present head of our secret police. The horror of the thing deeply impressed me, but the brutal, the idiotic, the utterly nonsensical stupidity of the thing impressed me much more.

We seem now to be tryingâ not to cure the ulcerous prison systemâ but to apply a little ointment to its sores. This is a trifle, but it is something, and it is due to the humane enterprise of Toynbee Hall. Mr. St. John Ervine has lectured to criminals on the drama, and if applause is any guide the lecture was a very great success. Then Mr. Lacey lectured on Plato's Republic, and Mr. Lacey also had a triumph. Then Mr. Fielden, a professor at the Royal College of Music, addressed our burglars, pickpockets, and would-be assassins on the history of music. He played some of the great nocturnes of Chopin, and was " heartily applauded."

I had horrid little doubts as I read about that lecture on Plato's Republic, and these little doubts grew to big doubts when I came to the great nocturnes of Chopin. Here we herd together " the scum of the population," and we subject them to a regime which must necessarily brutalise them and destroy all their finer sensibilities; and then we invite them to listen to music which requires for its appreciation not merely experience in listening to music but an inborn taste for music.

But the prisoners" applauded heartily." Well, of course they did. They would be only too delighted by any diversion from the senseless tedium of their lives. If the lecturer had stood on his head or if two cats had been put to gambol on the piano-keys, the enchanted prisoners would have applauded even more heartily. Let us have music in our prisons by all means, and plenty of it; for its influence upon the mind is probably superior to all other influences. And let us do the prisoners " good," if we can do it without ourselves being unimaginative prigs and highbrows.

We really ought not to say to the prisoners in effect: " We've got you. You are dying for want of diversion. You'll applaud anything on earth. And so you shall jolly well applaud what we like and not what you like." I consider it insulting to play the great nocturnes of Chopin before defenceless prisoners. I would endeavour merely to please them, without any conspiracy to do them " good." Because if I pleased them I should be doing them good.

I would get a vocalist to sing to them a selection of old English, Scottish, and Irish songs. The applause would bring the prison down.

The prisoners would laugh and they would cry. And I should at any rate be free from the ghastly reproach of deliberately trying to undo in an hour the harm which I was doing deliberately week by week and year by year.

The attitude of one sex to another is nowadays fundamentally changed in regard to what was once the most urgent of all matters, namely, of course, love,â at least so I am often told, and so I often read! The masculine attitude, according to the popular theory, has not altered. No! The young man, and indeed the middle-aged, is supposed still to be the seeker, the hunter, the devourer, the male whose possessive instincts insist on being satisfied. It is the young woman who has changed.

According to the popular theory the attitude of the modern young woman might be expressed thus:

"I am not what I was. In fact, beneath my exterior, which is more charming than ever before, I am so sternly altered you won't know me. Please, therefore, do not make the mistake of trying to practise any of your old devices. Once I lived solely for love and marriage. I dreamt about nothing but the ideal man: I had no aim but to be mistress of a home. But I am now quite otherwise. I have become a serious creature. I have higher and nobler interests than those of mere love. I am no longer foolishly sentimental. Generally I have a vocation and not seldom a profession. I can earn my living, and I do. I am more or less independent. I see life and I know it. My mind has been lifted up to view the world. And I have realised that I used to be rather silly in my mental demeanour towards such agreeable specimens of the other sex as I happened to meet. Love is not much after all. Can you expect my thoughts to be running after love when they are occupied with better and more interesting things? Can you give me any reason why I should become a domestic slave? My horizons are enlarged, and I am not in the mood for any nonsense."

For myself, I receive the report of the modern feminine attitude with caution. For I have not yet met with it in real life. There are a certain few girls who have little or no use for men or marriage, who feel no natural desire to look better when a man is observing them than when a woman is observing them. But there always were such girls, and such girls have their proper place and usefulness in every organised society. And that the percentage of them has increased I do not believe, because I can think of no reason why it should have increased.

Take the existence of an average girl who goes out into the world and works therein. Does she do it for a pastime? The answer is. No. People don't toil so many hours a day and submit to discipline and suffer the annoyances and nervous strain of a city journey night and morning, and keep on toiling and submitting and suffering month after month and year after year, simply for a pastime. Even an enthusiastic girl doesn't do that. Does she do it, then, from a sense of duty to the world, or to her country, arguing that everybody ought to help the general welfare.? The answer is again. No. Very few men, and still fewer women, have the sense of public duty developed beyond the sense of private advantage. If girls work in the same fields as men, they do so rather because they must in order to live, or because they can thereby attain a personal or family advantage beyond the mere means of existence.

People say that work is enjoyable for its own sake. It simply is not. No sane, well-balanced person enjoys work for its own sake. He, or she, may derive a secondary enjoyment from work that productively exercises a faculty. But all work, broadly considered, is a nuisance. Everybody except the queer person regards work as the means to an end, the end being either knowledge, or money and the exchanging of money for pleasure or power. If by a miracle all girl workers, or men workers either, could inherit a comfortable fortune, the business offices of London, New York, and Chicago would empty themselves more quickly than a theatre empties itself after a show. They would be deserted and forlorn between one sunrise and the next. The play would be definitely over.

The final purpose of the working girl in setting to work and keeping at work is, after she has provided for necessaries, to increase her luxuries: which chiefly means to make herself more attractive, and to lay by a relatively modest sum for emergencies and calamities. It cannot be doubted that she looks forward to the day when she will not have to work, or will have to work less, and will be able to enjoy herself more.

Further, no girls who take their share in the world's hard labour show the slightest sign of distaste for the society of men in circumstances favourable to romance? Do they when six, or whatever the hour for leaving-off may be, chimes on the office clock or the church clock, murmur to one another: " What a pity that the delightful day of toil is finished and that we are compelled by convention to mingle with men and give ourselves up to diversion! How much more pleasant it would be if we could shut out men and their desires and give ourselves to the discussion and contemplation of matters more earnest and nobler than the sentimental dalliance of the sexes! "â do they? To answer that they do not is an understatement.

Does a man find that in actual practice the modern independent or semi-independent girl is less disposed than any other sort of girl to explore with him the charming regions of sentiment? If he admires her, does she frown on him? If he suggests the restaurant, the theatre, the cinema, the ballroom, does she reply: " You ought to know that I have outgrown these baubles "? Does the youth of the two sexes dance less or does it dance more? Are the twilight and the moonlight any less popular to-day than they were fifty years ago? Have twilight and moonlight and the manoeuvres of the dance and the enlacing of arms ceased to have the usual fine healthy crop of conjugal consequences? Is it untrue to-day that the sums which a girl spends in heightening her attractiveness are a pretty sure index to her financial resources? Lastly, have girls decided that deliberately and consciously to exercise charm when a man comes along is an old-fashioned and undignified proceeding? I need not answer any of these queries. The answers are known to everybody.

The truth is, nature still exists.

I certainly do not count myself among those who assert that human nature never alters. I am convinced that it does alter, and almost always for the better. But it alters so slowly that no man lives long enough to witness in his lifetime such a fundamental change as is popularly attributed to the modern girl in her relations I with the modern man. A coral reef is built up in some thousands or tens of thousands of years, and I gravely doubt whether the development of human natureâ at any rate in its more important manifestationsâ is as rapid as that of a coral reef.

The great secret purposes of nature are principally assisted by the desire of the modern man to run after the modern girl and by the desire of the modern girl to do all she properly can to make him run after her. Are the great secret purposes of nature to be defeated or checked because the modern girl works in an office and gets wages? Nature is quite clever enough to use those wages in the furthering of the aforesaid secret purposes.

The tactics of the modern girl are profoundly rightâ much more so than her methods of reasoningâ because they spring from sane instincts so powerful and all-pervading that she seldom even notices them. And let there be no mistake about it.

I am tempted to go further and say that the desire of the girl to be married is still to-day, just as it was in the days before women went to business, smoked, and laughed at the mere notion of chaperones, decidedly stronger than the desire of the man to marry her. Women were the chief instruments of nature's plan in the previous age, and in my view they still are. It will be seen that I have travelled a long way from the popular theory that the modern girl has a tendency to hold off marriage, into which the modern man vainly tries to entice her; but I do not think that I have gone too far. Nor do I think that many men will disagree with my impression that man, while apparently the seeker, is still in fact, as of old, the sought. I should add that in this condition of affairs I see nothing derogatory to women. Rather the reverse.

Nevertheless the changed position and the consequent changed outlook of the modern girl have brought about appreciable, if minor, changes in the working of the ancient institution of betrothal and marriage.

In the previous age, if any reliance is to be placed on the best novels and the best memoirs of the period, the girl thought about almost nothing but marriage, and, aided by her mother, directed her energies mainly to that end, until achievement of the wedding altered the whole trend of her activities. She acted so partly because she had nothing else to do, and partly because home was a far more cramping and tedious and disciplinary place than it is to-day. Thus she had a stronger direct reason for plunging into marriage at the first opportunity, and this reason was reinforced by a graver fear of complete frustration if she should fail in the endeavour to mate herself. The modern girl has less reason to seek emancipation in marriage, for she is already considerably emancipated, and she is less disposed to hurry the process of marrying, because failure to marry does not now involve a fate that some persons apparently considered worse than death. This does not at all mean that her fundam ental instincts are different from those of her predecessor. It means that her new position enables her to exercise more care in the satisfaction of those fundamental instincts, and that she is less likely to satisfy them foolishly because, being a worker, she has less leisure to brood herself into an unhealthy state of mind about the tremendous subject.

It means also, that knowing more of the world and of men, she is a better and more realistic judge of men, and things, as they actually are. Hence she feels safe to pick and choose.

She does not say to herself: " I think I am in love with him or soon shall be; he has excellent points; and I may never get another chance so good," in the manner of hundreds of heroines in hundreds of old novels. Not a bit!

She says: " This affair interests me; but I am not so badly off; I am nobody's slave. I can keep myself. I know that men are not always what they seem. Therefore, although I am determined to marry, and want to marry more than I want anything, I will examine this par- ticular affair with coolness before allowing it to reach a higher degree of intimacy."

Such an attitude, while it would not denote any weakening of the instinct to marry, would undoubtedly tend to delay marriage and would in the long run raise the average age of marriage â with important consequences to society at large.

But wait a moment: to balance this new factor there are two other new factors.

First the economic factor, which perhaps more than any other influences the marrying age. The girl of to-day, if she chooses to keep her situation â and she often doesâ can make possible a marriage which otherwise would be economically impossible. Two incomes are better than one, and the girl has a double reason for contributing income to the joint enterprise; by so doing she will not only hasten its consummation, but she will safeguard to a certain extent that most precious possession, her independence. Here, then, is something which tends to lower the marrying age instead of raising it.

The second new factor consists in the immense widening of the modern girl's field of choice. She moves more freely in the world and she meets not merely far more men than her cooped-up predecessor, but far more sorts of men. Hence she has a far better chance of meeting the right man, and hence, other things being equal, she is likely to marry earlier than her predecessor.

It will be said that I have examined the marriage question only so far as it is influenced by the desires and the situation of the girl, and that it must be influenced also by the desires and the situation of the man. True. But my inquiry was limited to the girl's side, which I am persuaded is the more important and influential side of the matter. My argument was that the mighty institution of marriage is not going, and will not go, out of fashion because the modern girl has discovered something to take its place or to take the thousandth part of its place. This often expressed fear that girls are jibbing at marriage is just about as well grounded as the fear that girls are losing their feminine charm. It makes the judicious smile.

Since girls see more of men and more of life than their mothers did at their age, they have become wary. In other words, they are less apt to be rash and foolish in the great decisions. One leading result of this is the gradual decline of the specially Anglo-Saxon institution of the love-match. And not a bad result either!

At once many readers will be angry, and some very angry. What! Abolish love in marriage! What! Adopt the heartless " continental" system of the deliberately arranged marriage, the marriage of convenience! Well, nobody wants to abolish love in marriage, and nobody could. But we must understand what we mean when we say " love." The majority of love-matches are matches of passion which too frequently no practical consideration has been allowed to restrain. The partiesâ and especially the girlâ enter into them in a state of mind and body which is abnormal, and under the most astounding illusion. The illusion is that the abnormal state of mind and body is normal and will continue.

It won't. Not one passion in a thousand lasts, as a passion, more than three years. Few last, as passions, more than six months; an appreciable proportion do not survive the honeymoon. The passion may settle down into a solid and enduring calm affection; or it may wither into a tolerant mutual indifference; or it may degenerate into actual dislike. At best the disillusion is serious; at worst it is appalling. People laugh when letters of passion are read in the matrimonial courtsâ " My own darling pet little

Hugsy-Wugsy "â but they ought really to weep for the tragedy of the thing. The one conceivable advantage of the love-match pure and simple is that it does furnish a unique emotional experience. Whether that experience yields, even while it is in being, more happiness than unhappiness is a nice question which each person will probably decide on personal grounds. But it is certain that passion is not all beer and skittles.

Now the " heartless continental system" assuredly cannot claim to provide this unique emotional experience, with its delicious and its dreadful moments. On the contrary, for good or evil, it expressly avoids such experience. The parties are not in an abnormal state when they enter into the contract. The girlâ I speak more particularly of herâ is under no passional illusion. She does not imagine that her life is ready made. She knows that she has to build it up. And she sets about building it up. She may fail, of course; but on the other hand a solid and enduring affection may be reached, and very often is reached. At any rate since the material factors of the situation have been prudently studied and balanced beforehand, there is less chance of them poisoning the life of the heart than under the happy-go-lucky passional system.

Moreover the proof of the pudding is in the eating. Do continental marriages turn out on the average less satisfactorily than Anglo-Saxon marriages? They positively do not. Therefore, I welcome the decline of the love-match in Anglo-Saxon countries. For if in France, for example, " reason " in marriage has ruled too absolutely, in Britain, for example, " passion" has ruled too absolutely; and there is now some hope that we may be approaching the happy mean.

The point of the above is a remarkable illustration of the great and broad fact that girls are trying to look after themselves better than they used to do. Necessarily this implies that they are becoming the rivals of men in the struggle for the sweets of life. I do not refer to the rivalry of the sexes in the various professions and callings which make up the activity of a national existence. That particular rivalry is important in a material senseâ for women have already almost completely ousted men from certain fields of workâ but to my mind it is not so important as the general rivalry, which may be expressed thus:

In the opinion of women, men have hitherto had a better time than women. (Some men would attempt to deny this, but I do not think that it can be successfully denied.) Women are now determined to have as good a time as men. And since marriage is the supreme social institution, transcending all others in its daily-effect on all human beings who are either husbands or wives, women are specially determined that the sweets of marriage shall be more evenly divided in future. To speak bluntly, they are determined that in marriage there shall be a vast deal less subjection than there was.

Some, instead of saying " less subjection would say " less servitude " or even " less slavery." And I for one would admit that in employing these horrid words they were not speaking too strongly. Let us remember that not many years have passed since British married women were not allowed the control of their own property. Let us remember that until quite lately the Government when it collected income tax absolutely declined to recognise that women might have an income of their own.

And things are moving. Gone is the good old epoch when women had no political or social opinions of their own, when the wife said:

"Harry thinks " implying that naturally what Harry thought she must think, and when wives who did venture to contradict their husbands on any question more important than the proper number of minutes for boiling an egg were regarded as in danger of being unsexed! Wives are acquiring intellectual independence, happily for themselves and happily also for their husbands, for to live permanently with an echo is exceedingly bad for even the most saint-like husband. British wives have not, however, as yet got far in the process of acquiring intellectual independence. It is different in the United States, where the wife's intellectual independence is absolute, and is everywhere taken for granted, and you never perceive on the wife's face that apologetic expression so often remarked on the faces of wives in England, signifying: " Please do not think ill of me because I do not happen to see eye to eye with my husband on all the important topics of the day."

But then the intellectual independence of American wives has been quickened by the habit which American husbands have of looking on their wives as their official representatives in society, and indeed of expecting their wives regularly to act as such. If an American husband gets home at ten o'clock after a day spent in the arduous pursuit of money and finds his wife out of the house at a lecture, a concert, or a dance, he does not blame, he applauds her. She is representing him in the social world, and he will cheerfully carry on without wifely companionship until she returns. We are not like this in Britain, at any rate to the same extent, and probably never shall be and don't want to be; but we are moving along at our usual jogtrot. Meanwhile, despite progress achieved in the new rivalry, it cannot be contested that the majority of foreigners visiting Britain and studying its social conditions are simply amazed at the " submissiveness " of British wives. No doubt it is like their impudence to be amazed at the submissiveness of British wives, and British wives may resent the imputation and British husbands may object to the foreigner making trouble in the British household by his ill-timed criticism. But that is what foreigners think; and you may take it as a maxim that what foreigners think of us, whether pleasant or unpleasant, has some basis of truth in it.

You may also take it as a maxim that merely to claim, and pretend to exercise, intellectual independence is not enough. Intellectual independence involves individual ideas about things, and individual ideas cannot be obtained without study and reflection. Conversely, study and reflection are bound to result in intellectual independence. If wives feel a genuine interest in matters outside the narrow sphere of the home, and give themselves the pains of examining them for themselves, they will reach intellectual independence, and if each of them had forty husbands instead of one, forty husbands could not stop them from reaching it. If on the other hand they hanker after intellectual independence just for the sake of asserting themselves, they will produce a lot of friction and naught else. Everything has its price, and the price must be paid: the price of intellectual independence is intellectual activity. The wife who only reads the newspaper (as distinguished from glancing at the newspaper) when she can't find anything else to do, and still insists on her opinions, is asking for humiliation.

You will say: " Intellectual independence is all very well, but what about the other kind of independence, the financial, the material kind? Is there any progress there? " Well, according to my observation there isâ some. Here we are up against the ancient truth, deeply founded in the roots of human nature, that the person who pays the piper will call the tune. Unless a wife has a private incomeâ and few haveâ she will only arrive at the independent control of money for her own purposes by the favour of her husband. That, resources permitting, she ought to have the independent control of a certain amount of money is clear to the unbiassed mind, but in order to see this, nine husbands out of ten will have to get their eyes attended to. And perhaps some husbands are getting their eyes attended to. It is being more and more recognised that a wife renders services which, in a world based on economic principles, should receive remuneration either direct or indirect. No doubt the change is in part due to the fact that previous to marriage innumerable wives earned money and employed it independently; such women could not easily be treated as their mothers were treated. Common sense and right feeling would both revolt against it. Nevertheless many girls who abandon financial independence for marriage still go through bitter experiences.

Per contra, many wives are apt to forget, in the heat of modern rivalry, that they have a duty which goes beyond, and is at least as important as, the material duties connected with a home and a family. That duty is consciously to exercise charm. If man has to conquer by force and reason, woman has to conquer by charm. And by charm she can conquer. In charm she has an instrumentâ I will not call it a weaponâ in the use of which man cannot approach her, and she can use it as effectively whether she is nineteen years of age or fifty-nine. She must not disdain it. She often does disdain it. A man who provides week by week the material means of life for a household is entitled to expect that the mistress of the household shall put herself to the trouble of charming him. And heaven knows that the simple fellow is easily charmed!

If anyone objects that rivalry between the two sexes is regrettable, I very much agree. Rivalry in well-doing is admirable, but the sort of sex-rivalry now existingâ rivalry for the possession of privileges and power, a battle between the haves and the have-nots, and to some extent an attempt on the part of women to prove that they can be both women and men tooâ this sort of rivalry is bound to have some queer consequences. Do away with it, therefore? You cannot. And I doubt whether the abolition of sex-rivalry at this juncture, were it possible, would not work more harm than good.

The present generation has been born into a very exciting age. Even without the immense earthquake of the War the age would have been very exciting. It is an age of transition, and especially is it an age of transition for women. Women have advanced, and they will continue to advance until a period of stability has been reached; which period is assuredly not yet. But women have not advanced a single step without a definite fight and without having aroused a frequently bitter spirit of mutual rivalry. Very few people will be bold enough now to argue that the advance of women was not right or that it has gone too far. And looking back we can see that the opposition of the male sex was often quite unreasonable, and that the masculine predictions of disaster if women were allowed to do this or to do that show no sign of being fulfilled. Who, for example, would do away with women doctors or assert that they are not an extremely valuable institution? Yet the first women who insisted on being doctors were forced to lead lives which amounted to a martyrdom. (And all in the name of common sense!) And so the great struggle proceeded and is still proceeding. The fact is that the male sex has never yielded anything to the female sex without a battle, and sometimes without a regular pitched battle involving serious casualties. This has not been because men more than women are horrid pigs, dogs-in-the-manger, or odious beasts of any descriptionâ it has been because men are human, and it is not human to give up what you possess without some considerable altercation.

Sex-rivalry now and for years to come is inevitable. It is a condition of progress. It affects everything. And naturally it must influence the marriage bond. We have to make the best of it. In order to make the best of it, husbands and wivesâ and perhaps wives more than husbandsâ should continually remember its dangers. And as a fact that is what the wiser husbands and wives are already doing. The dangers have been perceived and precautions are being taken. Sagacious girls have begun to regulate their attitude and demeanour upon the maxim: " Let us have the minimum of rivalry and let us counteract unavoidable rivalry by the antidote of co-operationâ and charm." And sagacious young men have begun to observe this and to regulate their own attitude and demeanour accordingly.

An excellent reassuring symptom of the state of the sex-situation is to be seen in the marked decline of mannishness among girls. They claim the right to do all sorts of things that men alone used to do, but they do them in their own way. I am inchned to think that not for generations have women been more feminine, and more agreeably feminine, than they are at this hour.

I WITNESSED an English version of von Scholz's The Race with the Shadow at the Court Theatre, given by the Stage Society. The play was produced by Theodore Komisarjevsky, formerly producer and art-director of the Moscow State and Imperial Theatres; and special importance was attached by the committee of the Stage Society to this fact. I sat in row K of the stalls and there were seven rows behind me.

Mr. Komisarjevsky had evidently aimed at, among other things, realism in speech. The characters, for no dramatic reason, would stand for considerable periods with their backs to the audience; they would whisper; they would murmur; they would drop syllables and whole words; they would put their hands over their mouths. All very true to life; but carrying realism to excess, carrying it much further than the author or the scene-painter or the stage-manager carried it. The slowness of pace I could get accustomed to, after a few minutes, but I could not get accustomed to not hearing. Entire speeches were lost in the air between me and the stage, and various psychological details became incomprehensible through the vanishing of a key-word.

The first thing, on the stage, is to get oneself heard clearly by the audience without putting a strain on the average ear. This is probably a platitude, and yet at rehearsals of my own plays I spend half my time in reiterating it, and once I made a star actress very cross by telling her that it is useless to act magnificently until one is audible.

In the case of The Race with the Shadow, a very interesting night was about 50 per cent, ruined by Mr. Komisarjevsky's anxiety to attain realism of speech. He seemed to me (who could not produce a play to save my life) to have forgotten that no stage representation, and no part of it, can properly be realistic beyond a certain degree. It is and must be one enormous compromise with realism. Thousands of trifles have to be sacrificed in order to achieve a broad effect of truth. The West End stage is notorious for inaudibility, but this night was the most outrageous illustration of inaudibility that I have ever endured, even in the West End. I hurried to dressing-rooms and remonstrated with the admirable chief players. They were rightly alarmed, and promised with eagerness to reform, but in the next act they went on just as before. What the people at the nether end of the auditorium made of the piece I cannot imagine.

But the patience of pittites is amazing; it is heroic. For one reason or another about one-third of the accommodation in most theatres is merely vile. Either you are asphyxiated, or you are beaten by arctic winds, or your limbs are martyrised, or you can't hear, or you can't see; and the implied contract between management and playgoers is thus nightly broken.

Nevertheless no theatre has yet been burnt down by furious playgoers. I

You see those two young women coming forth from the boarding-house. Perhaps if you are by nature critical you do not think much of them; but I am here to tell you that they are worth looking at, that they are admirable self-creations, that indeed they are marvels of skill and ingenuity.

It has been stated that a woman cannot dress really well on less than ten thousand a year. Possibly. But these two girls keep themselves, they do not earn more than five pounds a week between them, they have saved the railway fares and the living expenses for their annual holiday, and in addition they have made themselves smart. This it is which is marvellous.

They are tremendously out to attract, and they do attract. (In this great matter they have understood the value of white on a sunny day, and it is sunny.) Watch them go on the pier, where flags are flying, penny-in-the-slot machines are clicking, and the band is playing. You might imagine that butter would not melt in their mouths, but you would be mistaken.

Now, you see those two young men, equally smart. Oh, regular dogs in their way! The two couples pass and re-pass. Will the white girls deign to glance at the smart young men? Not they. Apparently the young men do not exist for them. The white girls go back to the boarding-house for tea. But at night somehow, mysteriously, inexplicably, perhaps over the hazard of a slot-machine, these two couples have mingled into a foursome.

You ask me, suspicious, whether they have been introduced. Well, they have not. Only in certain circles do people have to be introduced, just as only in certain circles do people have to pay calls and leave cards. These two young women protect themselves, and maintain the conventions, by being together. Alone, neither of these would dream of not snubbing effectively any smart young man who had the audacity to advance.

The next day all four go for a walk. In the evening they dance. The day after they go for a walk and return in two separate pairs, and one pair (the girl with the thin ankles makes half of it) have now and then dropped from their continual back-chat into genuine seriousness, each trying to comprehend what the other really is.

And on the following day the girl with the thin ankles emerges from the boarding-house in a dream. She sees the contents-bills of the newspapers blazing with mighty world events, and she treats them as trifles. An illustrated advertisement in a picture paper is far more to her than the ruin of a great nation. As for the town, the apparatus of pleasure, the pier, the flags, the band, the sea itselfâ they are naught but the setting for her private business.

You protest that the silly little thing has lost her sense of perspective. Not at all. Hers is the true perspective. Her private business is the supreme business of nature, incalculably more important than anything else.

Guernsey is the great fruit-and-produce island, whose principal customer is England. Its surface is covered, and some of its beauty spoiled, by immense greenhousesâ greenhouses as large as railway terminiâ greenhouses that you would think could exist only in dreams, vast crowded prisons of forced plants. Its roads are patrolled by great motor-vehicles that do nothing but collect baskets of fruit and produce from the farms and disgorge the baskets on Whiterock Pier at St. Peter Port, capital of the State of Guernsey.

The most characteristic and vital phenomenon of St. Peter Port is baskets full of fruit and produce continually descending shoots into the holds of steamers. These baskets slither down, one running quietly after the next, all day and every day (except Sunday), monotonously, endlessly, maddeningly. You would think that if the inhabitants of the entire globe devoted their whole time to eating fruit and produce they could scarcely keep level with the incalculable contents of these steamers. Just as the people of certain parts of France live in and by and for wine, so the inhabitants of the very prosperous island of Guernsey live in and by and for fruit and produce.

I was standing on the Whiterock Pier and I beheld an enormous pile of baskets full of fruit, and. I thought I would examine the labels on the baskets and see where the magnificent fruit (plums) of which I had a glimpse through the wicker was going to.

Well, it wasn't going anywhere. It had come. It had come to Guernsey. It had come from Evesham in England to the fruit-island. I could at first hardly believe my eyes. I should have been less surprised to see coal unloaded on the quays of Newcastle. But my eyes were not mistaken. Presently the hundreds of packages were carried off the pier in motor-vans. It pays people to grow fruit round about Evesham, gather it, and send it by train to Southampton, unload it off the train on to a steamer, and dispatch the steamer to Guernsey, where the fruit is unpacked and sold at a profit!

This strange affair taught me a lesson about coming to hasty conclusions in such a complex and bewildering matter as overseas trade.

I know prominent persons in England who, if they infested Guernsey, would kick up a dreadful row about English competition and the necessity of safeguarding home industries, and who would put a duty on English fruit. Guernsey, however, does not do this. Nevertheless the fruit industry flourishes there. Indeed everything in Guernsey seems to be cheap except fruit. You can buy a decent cigar for less than you can buy a decent fig. Strange!

The " great" passenger shipping companies are marvellously exempt from Press criticism. (I need not go into the reasons for this.) All the public hears about the wonder-ships is an exciting tale of their vastness, their luxury, and their speed. Never a derogatory word! The wonder-ships are indeed wonderful, and they deserve much praise; but passengers in some of the very biggest of them, and passengers in any ship belonging to certain lines, will tell authentic tales of dirt, discomfort, bad service, and bad food. No daily paper would print these tales. I say nothing of the treatment of the crew.

Dirt, discomfort, bad service, and bad food do not, however, entail risk to life. What is much more important than these is the notorious neglect of owners of nearly all lines to adopt precautions for minimising the loss of life in case of accident. I have travelled by good lines and by bad lines, and I have never yet seen a boat-drill; I have never yet been told what boat I should seek in case of danger; and I have never yet even seen a cover taken off a boat. Swimming baths and ballrooms are excellent on board; but if there is a collision you cannot dance on the sea, and you are hkely to have more swimming than you desire.

It is obvious that boat-drills should take place on every voyage, that such boat-drills should be public, and that, above all, the passengers should be invited to interest themselves in this matter vital to themselves. It is obvious that everybody on board should know what he ought to do in a crisis. It is obvious that all crews, whether European or Oriental, should be thoroughly disciplined. It is obvious that no crew incapable of acting according to discipline in a crisis ought to be employed at all. Are these things done? They are never done. Why are they not done? Because it would cost a lot of money to do them? Not at all. They are not done because the directing minds are slack in this particular respect, being, no doubt, convinced that no accident can happen to their ships!

Accidents can and do happen to the largest ships, and will happen again. And the larger the ship the greater the danger in case of accident. You cannot appreciate the size of a very large ship while you are on board her. You can only realise it by getting into a row-boat and rowing under her side. You then perceive that you are rowing along a street of six or seven-storey buildings. The sight is not merely impressive; it is appalling. You see the life-boats high above you. Imagine being lowered in a boat from the roof of a lofty house to the ground. Imagine the house itself to be pitching and tossing, and the ground to be a heaving sea. And imagine some scores of boats, and some thousands of people all in an acute state of nerves. Then you will get a notion of what the shipwreck of an important liner can be like. And remember that a list of the ship to either side may put half the boats out of action!

At best, life-saving at sea is a desperate business. The least the directors of shipping companies can do is to make certain that all the life-saving apparatus is in order and that all the. human beings affected hy the risk are thoroughly-drilled. Directors who fail in this crucial matter with fatal results are worthy to be indicted for manslaughter, and they would be indicted for manslaughter if they were not so exalted. Many a chauffeur has suffered imprisonment for negligence far less culpable.

When a man, discouraged by some setback, says: " I'm no good," he doesn't mean it. He merely means that in his opinion there is a shght possibihty that he is not absolutely perfect. He expects his friends to contradict him with vigour and to slap him on the back, and say: " Oh yes, you are a great deal of good." And they generally do.

At the present time, Britain, the parent of sports, the games-master of the world, is saying, after a startling series of disasters, "I'm no good." And those enlightened and dismal citizens of hers who foresee the end of the British Empire in a cricket match, are telling her with much seriousness exactly why she is no good.

She is no good, they say, because she has become conceited and slack, and because she is far advanced in decay. The dear self-satisfied old creature, they sneer, was supreme when she had no rivals, but immediately anybody stands up to her fair and square, she collapses. Of course they don't mean it. Of course ancient Britain knows they don't mean it. And Britain and they expect the wide world of sports and games to reply in a reassuring sense.

But the wide world of sports and games is doing nothing of the kind. It is saying to Britain,â and you can see it in the foreign press north and south, east and west:

"You're quite right. You are done for." That is the difference between the imaginary-case of the discouraged man as above, and the real case of the island that invented cricket, football, golf, tennis, prize-fighting, and ping-pong. Yes, and even baseball.

Before, however, accepting the verdict of the world it might be well for Britain to inquire into the history of the matter, and to ascertain for sure whether she really has been beaten in what she was trying to do. If two combatants meet in conflict and one does something that the other is not trying to do, it does not follow that the second is defeated, much less disgraced.

The ruling or influential class in Britain was always addicted to games and sport. It always preferred a bruiser to a biologist, and a W. G. Grace to a Herbert Spencer.

It took games with the utmost seriousness. The rest of the world observed this, and observed also that the British Empire was continually growing both in size and in power. Further, the world heard that Waterloo was won on the playing-fields of Eton. And the world began to put two and two together, saying:

"A far-sighted race, these Britons! They have perceived that games constitute the finest physical and moral training for the young, developing all sorts of faculties that cannot be developed without games; and they have gathered the political and commercial harvest of their wisdom. We, too, will take games seriously."

(Part of the argument was false, for it is absolutely certain that Britain did not go in for games because good games mean good business. Britain went in for games because she had an instinct for games and enjoyed them. Nations do not become great by deliberately taking thought, but by responding to their instincts. Still, in the British example, games and Empire did go together.)

The successful are always imitated, though usually imitated in externals rather than in essentials. International sporting affrays were gradually established, and gradually Britain was equalled by her pupils, and now she is being surpassed by them. They determined to beat Britain, and naturally they succeeded.

But the point is that though Britain took games seriously she only took them seriously as games. With her the passion was to play; she wanted to win, but on the condition that a game remained a game and an end in itself. With her the supreme end was never to win. She said: " I shall win if I can, but my game shall not be my business, and the chief charm of my game for me is that it is a great lark." There were lots of things she simply would not do in order to win. She refused to make certain sacrifices, and she scorned to employ the whole of her brains in the affair. As for scientific organisation, the notion thereof was abhorrent to the sporting islanders. (It always was, in any connection.)

The situation could be summed up thus. Britain had an object in life, to play and sport. Her rivals had an object in life, to beat Britain in play and sport. Both objects were attained. As for the rivals, they were extremely in earnest, as new converts usually are. So their games were more than gamesâ and also less than games. They were not an end, but a means. The end was enormous. Teeth were set; brows were knitted; lives were devoted; money was lavished; science was utilised; specialisation was enforced. First-rate human beings got up in the morning with one idea in their heads; they went to bed with the same idea; and if they dreamt they dreamt about the same idea. Games lost the spirit of games; they ceased to be distractions and grew into vocations. The sequel was inevitable. The supremacy of Britain, which she had never sought, and never seriously sought to keep, was taken from her.

A terrific outcry has followed; a hundred doctors are prescribing a hundred different tonics for the overthrown giant, while a hundred prophets are all prophesying the same woe: physical and moral degeneration.

Meantime, Britain continues to play games. Indeed, she plays them more than ever, and those persons who assert that whereas Britons formerly-played games, nowadays they prefer idly to watch games, are merely being silly. All statistics and all observations go to show that, in spite of the vast crowds that watch games, the number of actual players of games increases amazingly and continuously. And if games are gaining in popularity, the good influence of games must be growing in proportion, and what was true of the British past should be still more true of the British future.

This does not mean that nothing is wrong with British games. Undoubtedly something is wrong. The island games are chiefly in the control of a few very autocratic bodies, whose influence is enormous, and, for the most part, these bodies cannot or will not understand that, as sport becomes more and more democratic, so it must breed games which are performances and players who are performers. The number of players increases, and therefore the raw material out of which great players can be made increases. The great players compete more and more among themselves. Skill is developed to such a point that inevitably the game is transformed into a performance, into a star-turn. The number of people interested in the game increases with the L i6i increase of players, and these people want to see the star-turns in exactly the same way as they want to see a circus or a music-hall show or hear a supreme soprano. They insist on seeing the star-turn. They cannot be kept out of the grounds. They are ready enough to pay to enter. Hence gates and gate-money and what is called the commercialisation of games,â a commercialisation which is quite unavoidable and which does not spring originally from any base motive.

The transformation of a game Into a performance is justifiable for two reasons. First, it gives an innocent and proper pleasure to large portions of the population; second, it keeps up the standard of play, and is a valuable means of education for the ruck of players. But, of course, it tends to create a class of players for whom the game is more than a gameâ or less than a game. For these players the game is a business, a profession, a livelihood. And whether they make money out of the game or whether they don't, they are professionals.

Now the authorities that rule over sports in Britain have always frowned at professionalism in games. They have not been able to scotch it, but they have done all they could to discourage it and to put a slur upon it, especially in the greatest traditional national gameâ cricket. In cricket the authorities have undoubtedly sacrificed efficiency to the spirit of snobbishness. A professional in their esteem cannot be equal to an amateur. A professional may be the finest potential captain that ever lived, but he will scarcely ever be permitted to captain a team if there is a single amateur in the team. Nor must a professional be adequately paid. He may be capable of drawing ten thousand people into a field to see him hit, but he must not get more than the wages of a carpenter. Why? Because he has fallen from grace. He has taken his game absolutely seriously, and devoted his whole life to it.

o This cast-iron attitude on the part of the authorities often gets them into difficulties, and they can only get out of the difficulties by pretending vigorously that certain notorious professionals are not professionals but merely amateurs. Thus a miserable atmosphere of make-believe and deceit is created. All which may be very noble and splendid, but it is not cricket. I do not suggest that the state of affairs is directly or solely responsible for the perfectly marvellous failure of England to win a single match against a colony with one-tenth of England's raw material to choose from. The last Australian team happened to be a menagerie of highly exceptional talents. But I do suggest that cricket will not flourish again as it might until the authorities undergo a change of heart. And I say that the same apphes to various other games. (Cricket, in fact, matters less than some other games because it has no world-importance.) I see no reason why in order to be a professional it should be necessary to lose caste and to suffer ridiculous social humiliation. After all, this is not the eighteenth century. And stern professionalism, whether paid or unpaid, is bound to conquer in the upper layers of games.

The attitude which is antagonistic to professionalism is, and must be, antagonistic to the essential factor in the attainment of the finest possible standard of play â namely, strictly scientific and strenuous organisation with a view not to a great lark but to a victory. The percentage of professionals to the total body of players need not be large, but the existence of a percentage, duly honoured and remunerated, is necessary if any game is to prosper fully. Without professionals, amateurs must deteriorate. Without scientific organisation a game may keep caste socially, but it is bound to lose caste as a game and to fall into inefhciency. In order that ten thousand games may satisfactorily be no more than games, it is unavoidable that a hundred games should cease to be mere games, and, becoming performances, partake of the nature of business. The day of the supremacy of amateurism and amateurishness is over. Britain will no doubt realise this fact long after the rest of the world has realised it, but she will realise it, and the reactionary mandarins of to-day will either mend their ways or be overthrown. Professionalism, the invasion of sport by the scientific or business spirit, may have a bad side. So has amateurishness.

o No development that may happen in the organisation of the very highest skill in games need affect, save beneficially, the general practice of games by the people at large. The average youth and maid and man and woman will go on playing with average skill, and with the proved beneficial effects, whether Britain wins championships or loses them. But even in the average circles there is still a great deal of organisation to be done. And among the chief needs in this respect is the organisation of sports and games for elementary-school children. All the public schools, and nearly all middle-schools, give quite as much attention to games as to science or letters. The same is true of certain universities. And the defence of this policy is that games have a high educational value, both morally and physically. It is strange that the persons responsible for the welfare of Britain, persuaded as they are of the aforesaid high educational value of games, have never provided for sports in the schools of the people. Lately the colleges of

Oxford have been lending their grounds to Oxford elementary-schools and also helping to fit the schools out with games apparatus. Here is one example that might well be followed elsewhere, not because it is good that the proper education of the mass of the young should depend on the charity of a few units here and there, but because such efforts provide an object-lesson for the nation at large.

It is wrong that every school in the island has not its own sports field with full equipment. And it would be equally wrong if, at the present moment, a group of educational madmen got hold of the House of Commons and insisted upon such sports fields being established instantly and universally regardless of cost. But when the high priests of state finance have returned to reason, and the budget has ceased to look like the dream of a lunatic who is convinced that two and two make fourteen,â then something serious will have to be done about the systematic teaching and practice of games in the schools of the people.

The recent tendency of our economical Government to charge the public for the privilege of entering picture galleries and museums which belong to the public has not met with universal approval. Why? Saving is always saving.

On a rough calculation it costs three millions a day to govern us, and by the strictest cheeseparing enough might be saved on galleries and museums to run the country for five minutes. Who shall sneer at five minutes? True, to make the public pay admission fees to see public treasures would keep poor people away. But poor people are a great nuisance in public buildings. The fact is that they must be watched by officials whose time might be passed more advantageously.

And there is no absolute need to spend the money obtained for admission fees on governing us still more. The money might be spent on purchasing fresh treasures of art. True, the large public would never see the fresh treasures, but the fresh treasures would be there for experts to gloat over, and that is of course the principal thing.

It seems to me that the new device for economising might be carried a lot farther. Is it not monstrous that people should be given free entry into our magnificent cathedrals and churches? Would it not be more proper that those persons who wish to commune with Heaven in the historical sacred edifices of this realm should put down first a silver coin and then be clicked through a turnstile? And we must not forget the splendid parks of London and of the provincial cities. Look at Hyde Park, which may well call itself the national park, vdth its rhododendrons, herbaceous borders, green lawns, dells, trees, and bands of music! How much longer shall we practise the wild, wasteful lavishness of letting citizens wander gratis in this expensive paradise? The citizens actually leave bits of paper lying about; they actually impair the grass by walking on it; and we have to maintain officials who devote their whole time to picking up the bits of paper and nursing the wounded grass back to health. Such a state of affairs is fantastic and grotesque, and should be altered immediately.

Nor should reform stop here. Admittedly Britain is the greatest country on earth, the best governed, the most free, the safest. Any Government that knew its business would make a charge to citizens for the privilege of being alive on this unique island. A shilling a day seems ridiculously cheap for such a privilege, when the cost of dying and being buried is as heavy as it is nowa- days. A shilling a day per head would give the Government considerably over seven hundred millions per annum to play withâ sufficient to pay the salaries of a couple of million more Government officials. No Government can have too many officials. Our present Government is asleep to vast and beautiful possibilities.

History is still not taught. It is only hinted at. Some of the hints may be pretty plain, even illuminating; but the whole story is never told. The method of history-teaching may be likened to the method of a gossip, at once indiscreet and cautious, who gives glimpses of a dark social story at a dinner-party. You want the whole tale; you don't get it.

Of course the teaching of history has improved. In England J. R. Green has the credit, no doubt rightly, of having improved it. His History of the English People, and especially his Short History oj the English People (with the emphasis on the " people "), marked an epoch, creating a new popular conception of history, and destroying the notion that battles, insurrections, and royal accessions and demises constitute the only worthy material of history. Green wrote very badly; his pages are a congested mass of cliches, highly repellent to a fastidious literary taste. Also he was a sentimentalist through and through. Nevertheless he accomplished something, namely, a truer perspective than any previous popular 1 This heralding essay was vrritten and published before the first publication of Mr. H. G. Wells's An Outline of History. The prodigious, and in America the unique, success of the astounding work is a matter of common knowledge.

historian. And he wrote a complete history of England.

But is Green anywhere studied in his totality? Not, I think, in any educational establishment. In all educational establishments the terrible " period" system of history teaching obtains before any other system. You take a particular period; and the period may be chosen by hazard, by the caprice or prejudice of a master, by the exigencies of examinations, or for " practical " reasons which have no connection whatever with the teaching of history. And when one period is " done," another period is chosen in just the same irrational way as the first period. Few schoolboys have not experienced the sensation of leaping prodigiously backwards and forwards in English history according to the whim of some unknowable higher power.

Nor is this the worst of the affair. History in schools is not regarded as a major subject. In the best public schools in England it may and does happen to a boy of seventeen that he no longer studies history. He has finished with history for the rest of his learning years. The most educative of all subjects, the subject which more than any other is essential to wise citizenship, is henceforth forbidden to him. Probably it is not too much to say that no boy leaves school with a coherent outline in his head of the evolution of British civilisation. If he leaves school with any leading historical idea at all, it is the idea that Britain is somehow the centre of the universe and that all extra-British history is of secondary importance. In the matter of perspective he is not much better than the young lady of the fifties, for whom education meant instruction in deportment, embroidery, and the rivers of Europe in their order. He has not got the slightest imaginative hold of the fact that England is an inconsiderable and peculiar island lying off a great continent, and that the great continent itself is the least of the continents. He is exquisitely incapable of perceiving the tragic and mischievous awry-ness of the philosophy of Rudyard Kipling.

A smau percentage of schoolboys go to universities, and a small percentage of those who go to universities specialise in history. Exactly upon what system they learn I do not know, but I believe I am not wrong in affirming that they do not learn historical perspective in the world-sense. The tendency is always to specialise before generalising. The adolescent historical student seldom or never acquires from his professors any sufficient information about the relation between his selected field and the whole domain of historical knowledge. His light is a candle on a moor in a dark night. Even his professors, so far as I can judge from occasional inquisitions into their works, are but imperfectly seised of the basic truth that you simply cannot understand the history of China without keeping an eye on the sequence of events in Peru.

In my young days there used to be a maxim, much admired in Mutual Improvement Societies, to the effect that you ought to aim at learning something about everything and everything about something. The first half of this very wise saw has apparently been ruled out. The Greeks had an amazing gift for prophetic symbolism. Foreseeing Oxford, they represented Clio with a half-opened scroll in her hand. Delicious people, the Greeks! Thucydides didn't half appreciate them.

Thucydides, I am informed and believe, was the greatest historian that ever lived. He was, however, unacquainted with Darwin, and he dealt with trifles. They may have been important trifles, but in the evolution of the entire human race they were trifles, mere episodes in an epic immensely vaster than Thucydides could even conceive. This is what the average man of taste and intelligence feels when he emerges " educated" from the seats of learning. I want to bring forward the case of the average man of taste and intelligence. He soon perceives the defects of his training and the gaps in his knowledge. He is not a monomaniac about history. But he comprehends the value of history; he is ready to devote a portion of his spare time to it, and he would hke to use his hours scientifically to the best advantage. He has picked up, somehow, one or two leading scientific principles, and there is in him a sound instinct to submit all phenomena to the test of those principles. He has an honest desire to get rid of the prejudices whose existence in himself he assumes.

Quite probably he has had dramatic glimpses of the possibilities of intellectual freedom. Thus he may have read the Hammonds' book on the Town Labourer, which has opened vistas that he did not dream of when he humbly enjoyed Macaulay's intoxicating Victorianism; or he may have come across Spencer's Introduction to the Study of Sociology, which has permanently affected his old receptive attitude towards leading articles in daily papers. Or he may have read the regretted Payne's wonderful introductory pages to the Cambridge Modern History, which have quickened his scarce-born imagination and engendered in him a wild longing to escape from the wire cage of his ignorance to a high mountain with a view of the whole of space and the whole of time. He wants to know. He wants to be able to indulge in the supreme pastime of putting two and two together.

But, mind you, he is human. He has other interests. He may be keen on billiards. He does not intend to be a martyr of knowledge. He looks around for help. He does not look far, perhaps not farther than the publishers' advertisements. Suppose that his ambition is modest, confined to a wish to obtain a coherent view of the annals of his own country. He soon discovers that nearly all the so-called histories of England are only histories of comparatively brief periods, or that, if they deal with long stretches of years, they deal only with limited aspects of those stretches. (Thus Gardiner takes ten volumes to describe 2 per cent, of the two thousand odd years of what may be called English history. Thus Hunt and Poole's big co-operative affair in twelve volumes is specifically confined to " politics.") His need is for a comprehensive monograph. Where can he put hands on it? Of Green I have already spoken. Apart from scholastic text-books and such efforts as Gilbert Chesterton's intensely prejudiced political tract, what is there, unless it be the estimable Franck Bright's History in five manageable volumes? Franck Bright has no touch of fire; no elegance; no charm. He writes like a cab-horse; but he is complete; he is fair; he informs pretty accurately, and he is the enemy of reaction. He may be as bad as you pleaseâ he is the best and usefuuest thing extant for the average man of taste and intelligence!

But suppose that the man's ambition is not modest. Suppose that he wishes to obtain a coherent view of the history of the globe. There are huge compilations, such as Helmolt's, and Ratzel's. Do not imagine that the average man of taste and intelligence is going to hack his way through these. He is not. He must be amused and charmed while learning. That is to say, he demands, not a compilation, not a Harrods Stores, but a work of literature; indeed, a work of art. He may or may not have heard of such a fine book as Reade's Martyrdom of Man; but if he gets it and reads it, he will not get and read what he is really after, for in the very title the author shamelessly displays the enormity of an overmastering prejudice. The average man of taste and intelligence has too much poise to regard the evolution of the human race as chiefly a martyrdom. The fact is that the aforesaid man will not find what he wants anywhere, because it does not exist.

Having digested this sad fact, he may decide to limit his ambition to relatively modern times, and to tackle the Cambridge Modern History. A hundred to one the Cambridge Modern History will beat him off with great loss. It, too, is a compilation. It is heterogeneous. It is not informed by leading ideas. Much of it is unreadable. And it is too long. A finer work is the Histoire Generale, edited by Lavisse and

Rambaud, which begins at the fourth century and ends at the twentieth. But this also is a compilation, and extremely uneven. And it is too long, too long. After about a year's reading, I reached the end of the eleventh century, with over 90 per cent, of the work unexplored. I went no further, for, after all, my vocation in life is not to read history. And to-day, on the downward slope of my existence, I am still without any sort of coherent view of the totality of the world's history. There are thousands like me. There are probably not a thousand men in the whole world unlike me in this respect. The fault is not ours. The fault is that of the historians, who have not deigned to meet a notorious, a widespread, an urgent, and a vital demands

But hope shines. For some years past Mr. H. G. Wells has been preaching the importance of universal history in education. He has been preaching that history is one and indivisible, and that to chip pieces off history and offer them without first showing clearly their relation to the original block is a blunder whose consequences are very prominent in the present state of society. Mr. Wells wrote at the end of the War: " There can be no peace now, we realise, but a common peace in all the world; no prosperity but a general prosperity. But there can he no M common peace and prosperity without common historical ideas. Without such ideas to hold them together in harmonious co-operation, with nothing but narrow, selfish, and conflicting nationalist traditions, races and peoples are bound to drift towards conflict and destruction."

If the student of Mr. Wells's works asks where these words are to be found, the answer is that they are not to be found. They have been written, but not yet published. They are taken from the Introduction to The Outline of History, of which Mr. Wells is the author. Not a history of this or of that; not any particular aspect of history; but history, the comprehensive history of the globe, in all its main aspects.

Mr. Wells's work does not begin with the beginning of any tribe or nation. Still less does it begin with the Renaissance, the discovery of America, the rise of Charlemagne, or any such landmark. It begins with the earliest period of geological time, not less than eighty million years ago. It comes up to date. It provides a perspective in which the diplodocus and the latest opportunist statesman occupy their right relative places in the earthly scheme.

It is manageable by the average man of taste and intelligence. It runs to about four hundred thousand words (the same length as the longer novels of Dickens). It will first appear in parts; but there is no reason why ultimately it should not be sold, with all its illustrations and maps, in one volume, for, at most, half a sovereign. It can be read and understood by the plain man in the spare hours of a month. It is not a compilation, but a homogeneous work of literature. It exists as an artistic entity.

To conceive such a task for oneself was a powerful act of imagination. To begin it showed superlative courage. To finish it worthily is a truly astonishing achievement. Mr. Wells felt acutely the need of the work. He determined to supply it. True, he is not an expert historian! True, he may know little of " original sources "! But he is an expert in the co-ordination of phenomena. He is probably the greatest living expert in the scientific use of the imagination. His mind is scientifically organised. All his books, even the most fantastic, are based on the principles of science. Also he can write. No necessity to emphasise the point. He can write. Hence he can be read. Finally, he has had the wit to get his work, while it was in the making, overlooked and criticised by first-rate experts in the various divisions of it; so that no serene highness of a specialist will be able grandly to dismiss the thing as a novelist's circus-performance. If Mr. Wells accomplishes no more than a demonstration to historians that the whole of history can be somehow interestingly handled by one man within a reasonable space, he will nave cut a pathway. He will have served the cause of civilisation. But I apprehend that he will have accomplished more than that, and I anticipate the publication of the Outline as a notable event.

It was.

This morning we shall all cease work or play, and meditate upon the heroism and the tragedy of the War. The overcoatless ex-soldier will cease begging his bread in the gutter of Regent Street, and the maimed warrior will cease selling chocolates, in order to meditate upon the heroism and the tragedy of the War. A solemn two minutes! It is right that we should so meditate; for we are apt to forget that if heroes were cheap and plentiful, if there were five, six, or seven million heroes, they were none the less heroes, and none the less worthy of our most pious gratitude.

But while we are pondering over the dreadful and magnificent past, we should do well also to think clearly about the practical aim of those immense campaigns whose victorious conclusion we now celebrate. Their aim was to abolish militarism and the menace of the gun. To-day is the fourth Armistice Day. Heaven knowsâ the Chancellor of the Exchequer certainly doesn't â how much we shall spend this year on preparing for fresh wars; but, anyhow, last year we spent jf230,429,000 to this pleasant end. Income tax is still 6s. in the pound, super-tax is still anything up to 9s. in the pound. We grudge milk to babies, we starve children of elementary education, the country is ridden with hunger and idleness and cold, we put the brake on commerce and social relations so as to save 6 d. in the Post Office; but at the fourth Armistice Day we are grandly spending millions every week in preparing for future wars.

Matters are not improving, they are getting worse. " This way to catastrophe " is painted plainly on the signposts of the road along which we are travelling. And we travel fatalistically straight forward.

Everybody knows that war is idiotic, futile, calamitous, and settles nothing. And yet nearly everybody says, "There must always be war." Why must there always be war? In past days people no doubt said, "Brides must always be won by knocking girls on the head and carrying them off senseless. Evidence must always be obtained by torture. Christians must always murder each other in the name of Christ. Little children must always work eighteen hours a day â because human nature will always be like that." Well, they were wrong. Human nature did not continue to be like that.

War is contrary to common sense, and it is therefore absolutely certain that the institution of war will one day be ridiculed and shrivelled out of existence. Whether that day shall arrive in our time, or long after we are ruined and dead, depends on ourselves. It depends on you and me and the ordinary fellow next door. Human nature does change, and all history proves that it changes. Just try to do to-day some of the things that human nature approved of even only a century ago, and you will quickly find out whether human nature changes or not!

How does human nature change? By the action of the individual. It changes by you thinking straight and so changing your nature, and me thinking straight and so changing my nature. It does not change by each of us waiting for the other to begin. Human nature will change in its attitude to war by casting out fear. War is not the product of courage; it is the product of fear. Hence the insane maxim that if you want peace you must prepare for war. If you prepare for bankruptcy, you will have bankruptcy; if you prepare for war you will have war; and equally if you prepare for peace you will have peace.

But the risks, the awful risks, of disarmament!. Of course, there will be risks, though they will infallibly be far less awful than the risks of our present pohcy of arming. The indispensable preliminary to peace is courage to confront the risks, and faith to beheve that public opinion (your opinion and mine) can be strong enough to stop guns from going off. It can be strong enough, you know. And a dim, vague notion to that effect is gathering force throughout the world and exhibiting itself quite bravely in the shape of a Disarmament Conference at Washington.

And the populations are actually taking notice! The arrangements for reporting the Washington Conference are nearly as elaborate as those for reporting the Landru trial. I do not say this cynically, but with serious satisfaction, as is fitting on the fourth Armistice Day. I count the general interest in the Washington Conference as a sign that the workless workman, the pinched housewife, and the individual who pays away nearly a third of his income for the privilege of being misgoverned, have begun to perceive that human nature has just got to be changed. The Conference may failâ many expect that it will; a few hope that it will. But even if it does, the next one won't. Public opinion will have been educated.

I WENT into a certain small concert hall to hear a chamber concert in the same fine free spirit as Kipling's fellow " went into a public-house to get a pint of beer." And this is the right spirit. The hall was marvellously and outrageously ugly. I have been to that hall dozens of times, and its extreme ugliness always shocks me afresh. The point arises: Can a person of taste and sensitiveness properly enjoy music in such a painful environment? Not that the small hall in question is much uglier than any other small concert hall in the West End. It is not. There is no small concert hall that is not architecturally offensive. And, with one exception, there is no large concert hall that is not architecturally offensive. The exception is the Central Hall at Westminster, which is beautiful and enables you to withstand even ballad concerts.

Well, I went into the hall. The audience was fairly large, decidedly larger than the average audience at the four or five hundred musical entertainments given in that hall annually; that is to say, the hall seemed to be about three-quarters full, and was in fact about half full. The audience consisted in the main of ugly, Calvinistic, peculiar or superior people. Why are the frequenters of serious concerts so alarmingly ugly, and why do their features usually denote harsh intellectuality and repudiation? Why have they the air of mummies who have crept out of the pyramids in order to accomplish a rite? Why have they not the air of having come into a public-house to get a pint of beer? I shall have more faith in the thesis that the English are a musical nation when I see in the features of audiences an adventurous look indicating a secret feeling that they ought not to be there, instead of a solemn, haughty look indicating a secret assurance of entire righteousness.

Still, this audience suited the architecture of the hall. I wanted to laugh at it, but the thick moral atmosphere choked me. I should have preferred even the thin atmosphere of those family parties, called concerts, given by aspirants to fame and to pupils, of which probably at least a hundred are given in that same hall every yearâ concerts where the applause is candidly a claque and bears no relation whatever to the quality of the performance.

Well, I estimated the audience, and the concert began. The artists were a justly famous foreign string quartet. They played admirably. They played as well as the Philharmonic Four or the L. S. Q., and that is saying something. They started off with a Haydn. It was that quartet in which one of the memorable themes is tee â teetee â te â te â te â TEE, tee â teetee â te â te â te â 33JL. (There are about a million classical quartets with this theme, but everyone will be able to distinguish the one I am alluding to.) Joachim loved this quartet. I heard him love it at a Saturday Pop. at the Piccadilly Hotel over thirty years ago. But my notion is that it ought to have been interred with Joachim. It awakens no response in me. It makes me wonder whether Haydn ever knew what the French Revolution was. All honour to Haydn for having congealed the symphony; and I don't mind helping to play either his symphonies or his quartets in four-hand unpianistic piano transcriptionsâ it is a bit of a larkâ but that a distinguished foreign quartet should get passports to England and come to England and hire a hall and advertise themselves in order to play a Haydn quartet struck me as monstrous. I am convinced that the day is coming when Papa Haydn will be spoken of as we now speak of Diabelli or Mendelssohn or Spohr or Clementi.

My companion said to me, "Can't you sit still? " I said, "No, I'm damned if I can! " The performance was admirable, which made it all the more exasperating. Well, it finished. The applause was Haydnesque.

Then came a Beethoven quartet. I can never remember keys, I can only say that its number was well into three figuresâ according to the numeration of the higher criticism of Beethoven, which is quite possibly all wrong. Anyhow, the quartet was indubitably " late." To hear it brought to my memory all the mad, destructive attacks which have recently been made on Beethoven by those uncomfortable infants who won't let music rest in its classical congealment. And awful suspicions presented themselves to me: " Can there be anything in such abominable attacks? Did Diaghilev, though a gaffeur really give some hint of a truth? Can a god be incoherent? Does the world revolve?"

During this quartet a musical critic sat down near me and carefully perused The Sackbut. When he had done reading The Sackbut, and before the end of the quartet, he departed again. I thought: " His article will probably be absurd, but he is a better critic than I had imagined."

An admirable performance, but I was once again bored. Bored by an admirable performance of a late Beethoven quartet? Yes. My fault, of course. Still, there it is. You can say what you like about me except that I am not intelligently interested in music. I am. For a rank amateur I have had vast experience of listening to music. I have travelled specially from Paris to London, out of pure artistic curiosity, to hear a new symphony. Yes, and I have attended festivals of British music. And if I am bored it is not I alone who am to blame.

After the Beethoven quartet, I leaned over to a lady in front of me who was sitting by herself. I asked her: " What are you here for? " She said: " I thought I would come and hear some music." " Are you bored.? " " Horribly." " Don't you feel as if you would sooner be at the Palladium? " " I certainly do," she said, with enthusiasm.

The third and final item on the programme was another classical quartet. Three of us left before it started. We had to. We had no other engagement, but we just had to leave, or we should have begun to recite Dante's Pur-gatorio aloud.

That concert failed, so far as we were concerned, on its programme. I do not wish here to generalise, or to suggest remedies. But I must record my opinion that foreign artists, in choosing their programmes, do misapprehend the British public. At that concert the programme sinned in one way. At the opening concerts of Hoffman and Heifetz, for example, the programmes sinned in quite another way. The first way is by intimidation, the second is by something that resembles insult; and I don't know that there is anything to choose between them.

Though I may occasionally get terrible shocks of disillusion thereat, I immensely prefer the adventuous programmes of our most alive British artists, whether in solo work or concerted. Much new music is simple rot, but at any given period much new music was simple rot. And if any mandarin denies that new music is interesting, and very interesting, and often very interesting, and sometimes more interesting than any old music except Bach, Mozart, and Chopin, I respond that I am not a mandarin, and that I do not agree with him. At the present moment I would sooner go to hear Hoist's Planets and Strauss's Rosenkavalier than anything in the whole literature of music.

Well, I went to the Palladium. No sign there on the faces of the audience that they imagined they were doing a duty to art, or proving themselves the favoured of Heaven! But there was the good sign of the night out. I heard Ella Shields sing her celebrated song, "Burlington Bertie " (who rose at eight-thirty). It was a distinguished performance. I would rank Ella Shields as an artist appreciably above 95 per cent, of the artists whom I have heard at serious concerts in the last ten years. It is a wide world, and I wish the shepherds of the musical valley would realise this.

The fame of James Joyce was founded in this country mainly by H. G. Wells, whose praise of A Portrait of the Artist as a Toung Man had very considerable influence upon the young. For although the severe young spend much time, seated upon the floor, in explaining to each other that H. G. Wells is and must be a back number, he can do almost what he likes with them. I read A Portrait of the Artist as a Toung Man under the hypnotic influence of H. G. Wells. Indeed, he commanded me to read it and to admire it extremely. I did both. I said: " Yes, it is great stuff." But in the horrid inaccessible thickets of my mind I heard a voice saying: " On the whole, the book has bored you." And on the whole it had; and with the efflux of time I began to announce this truth. There are scenes of genius in the novel; from end to end it shows a sense of style; but large portions of it are dull, pompous, absurd, confused, and undirected. The author had not quite decided what he was after, and even if he had decided he would not have known how to get it. He had resources, but could not use them. He bungled the affair, and then threw his chin up and defied anyone to assert that he had not done what he did in the way he did solely because he wanted to do precisely that thing in precisely that way. A post facto pose with which all creative artists, and some others, are experientially acquainted.

A year or two later one of the intellectual young exhibited to me a copy of The Little Review, which monthly was then being mentioned in the best circles. I think this must have been in the period when even Mr. Middleton Murry was young. T he Little Review contained an instalment of James Joyce's Ulysses, I obediently glanced through the instalment and concluded that it was an affected triviality which must have been planned in what the French so delicately call a chalet de necessite. I expressed this view, and the intellectual young concurred therein; but I seemed to detect in the concurrence a note of mere politeness to the grey-haired. Hence, recalling the time when I laughed at Cezanne's pictures, I wondered whether there might not be something real in the pages after all.

And then the other day, opening La Nouvelle Revue Frangaise, I beheld blazing on its brow an article by Valery Larbaud entitled " James Joyce." I was shaken. La Nouvelle Revue Frangaise is in my opinion the finest literary periodical in the world. Valery Larbaud is a critic whom it is impossible to ignore. He is neither old nor young. He is immensely experienced in imaginative literature, and a novelist himself. He has taste. His knowledge of the English language and English literature is only less peculiar and profound than his knowledge of the French language and French literature. He is, indeed, a devil of a fellow. He probably knows more about Walter Savage Landor and Samuel Butler than anybody else on earth. He and Leon Paul Fargue are the only persons on earth who understand the verse of St. Leger Leger. He once amazed and delighted me by stating, quite on his own, that the most accomplished of all the younger British poets was Edith Sitwell: a true saying, though I had said it before him. And here was Valery Larbaud producing a long article on " James Joyce," and La Nouvelle Revue Frangaise giving it the place of honour! At this point, if I was A. B. Walkley, I should interject that that rrcavail donne furieuse-ment a fenser, and, if I were Mr. Clive Bell, that that had made me exclaim (in French) Mon Dieu! What I actually did say was something other.

Valery Larbaud's article was, according to his wont, exhaustive. It contains a comprehensive account of James Joyce from the creation to the present day, and in particular a full analysis and final estimate of Ulysses. And the conclusion of it is that Ulysses is a masterpiece, considered, shapely, and thoroughly achieved. I was left with no alternative but to read the thing. I saw the book at the house of a friend, and I said: N

"You have just got to lend me this." She lent it to me. It looks like a quarto, but it is an octavo: over two inches thick; 730 pages, each of a superficies of seventy square inches; over half a million words; and so precariously broche that when you begin to read it in bed it at once disintegrates into leaves, largely Sybilline. However, I read it. Perhaps some pages here and there I only inspected, but, roughly speaking, I did read it. And as I finished it I had the sensation of a general who has just put down an insurrection.

Much has been made of the fact that the author takes more than seven hundred big pages to describe the passage of less than twenty hours. But I see nothing very wonderful in this. Given sufficient time, paper, childish caprice, and obstinacy, one might easily write over seven thousand pages about twenty hours of life. A young French author once dreamed of a prose epic in many volumes, of which the first one was to be entirely devoted to the hero's journey in a cab from his home to the railway station. And why not? Certainly a book to a day need not be excessive. But it all depends on the day chosen. There is no clear proof that James Joyce chose for his theme any particular day. He is evidently of a sardonic temper, and I expect that he found malicious pleasure in picking up the first common day that came to hand. It happened to be nearly the daihest day possible. (If he had thought of it he would have chosen a day on which the hero was confined to his bed with a colique seche.) The uninstructed reader can perceive no form, no artistic plan, no " organisation " (Henry James's excellent word) in the chosen day.

But the uninstructed reader is blind. According to Valery Larbaud, the day was very elaborately planned and organised. James Joyce loved the Odyssey in his youth, and the spirit of Homer presided over the shaping of the present work, which is alleged to be full of Homeric parallels. It may be so. Obviously Valery Larbaud has discussed the work at length with the author. I should suspect the author of pulling Valery Larbaud's leg, were it not that Larbaud has seen with his own eyes the author's drafts. They consist of notes of phrases meant to remind the author of complete phrases; the notes are crossed out by pencil marks of different colours; and the colour indicates the particular episode into which the phrase has been inserted. This method of composing a novel recalls Walter Pater's celebrated mosaics of bits of paper each holding a preciosity. It is weird, but it does demonstrate that the author laboured on some sort of an organised plan.

I therefore concede him a plan, successful or unsuccessful. And in doing so I must animadvert upon his lamentable lack of manners. For he gives absolutely no help to the reader. He behaves like a salesman in an old-fashioned, well-established, small West-End shop, whose demeanour seems to say to you as you enter: " What! Here's another of 'em. I'll soon put him off. Now what in hell do you want, sir? " Nothing is easier than for an author to help his reader; to do so involves no sacrifice of principle, nor can it impair the value of the book. A writer writes not merely because he is interested, but also because he desires to interest. A sound book ought to be a fair compromise between author and reader. James Joyce, however, does not view the matter thus. He apparently thinks that there is something truly artistic and high-minded in playing the lout to the innocent and defenceless reader. As a matter of fact, there isn't. In playing the lout there is something low-minded and inartistic. Ulysses would have been a better book, and a much better appreciated book, if the author had extended to his public the common courtesies of literature. After all, to comprehend Ulysses is not among the recognised learned professions, and nobody should give his entire existence to the job.

A more serious'objection to the novel is its pervading difficult dullness. There is always a danger that short quotations may give a misleading and unfair impression of a work, or even of a chapter in a w ork; but I must risk the following extract, which I have conscientiously chosen as representative:

"Making for the museum gate with long windy strides he lifted his eyes. Handsome building. Sir Thomas Deane designed. Not following me?

"Didn't see me perhaps. Light in his eyes.

"The flutter of his breath came forth in short sighs. Quick. Cold statues; quiet there. Safe in a minute.

"No, he didn't see me. After two. Just at the gate.

"My heart!

"His eyes beating looked steadfastly at cream curves of stone. Sir Thomas Deane was the Greek architecture.

"Looking for something L"

Scores and hundreds of pages are filled with this kind of composition. Of course, the author is trying to reproduce the thoughts of the personage, and his verbal method can be justifiedâ does indeed richly justify itself here and there in the story. But upon the whole, though the reproduction is successful, the things reproduced appear too often to be trivial and perfectly futile in the narrative. I would not accuse him of what is absurdly called " photographic realism." But I would say that much of the book is more like an official shorthand-writer's " note " than a novel. In some of his moods the author is resolved at any price not to select, nor to make even the shortest leap from one point of interest to another. He has taken oath with himself to put it all down and be hanged to it. He would scorn the selective skill in such a masterpiece of narrative technique as Esther Waters (whose brilliance only experts can fully appreciate). He would probably defend himself, and find disciples to defend him. But unless the experience of creative artists since the recorded beginning of art is quite worthless, James Joyce is quite wrong-headed. Anyhow, with his wilfulness, he has made novel-reading into a fair imitation of penal servitude. It is not as if his rendering of life was exhaustive, or had the slightest pretension to be exhaustive. The rendering is extremely and ostentatiously partial. The author seems to have no geographical sense, little sense of environment, no sense of the general kindness of human nature, and not much poetical sense. Worse than all, he has positively no sense of perspective. But my criticism of the artist in him goes deeper. His vision of the world and its inhabitants is mean, hostile, and uncharitable.

He has a colossal " down " on humanity. Now Christ, in his all-embracing charity, might have written a supreme novel. Beelzebub could not.

Withal, James Joyce is a very astonishing phenomenon in letters. He is sometimes dazz-lingly original. If he does not see life whole he sees it piercingly. His ingenuity is marvellous. He has wit. He has a prodigious humour. He is afraid of naught. And had Heaven in its wisdom thought fit not to deprive him of that basic sagacity and that moral self-dominion which alone enable an artist to assemble and control and fully utilise his powers, he would have stood a chance of being one of the greatest novelists that ever lived.

The best portions of the novel (unfortunately they constitute only a fraction of the whole) are superb. I single out the long orgiastic scene, and the long, unspoken monologue of Mrs. Bloom which closes the book. The former will easily bear comparison with Rabelais at his fantastical finest; it leaves Petronius out of sight. It has plenary inspiration. It is the richest stuff, handled with a virtuosity to match the quality of the material. The latter (forty difficult pages, some twenty-five thousand words without any punctuation at all) might, in its utterly convincing realism, be an actual document, the magical record of inmost thoughts thought by a woman who existed. Talk about understanding " feminine psychology ". I have never read anything to surpass it, and I doubt if I have ever read anything to equal it. My blame may have seemed extravagant, and my praise may seem extravagant; but that is how I feel about James Joyce.

It would be unfair to the public not to refer to the indecency of Ulysses. The book is not pornographic, and can produce on nobody the effects of a pornographic book. But it is more indecent, obscene, scatological, and licentious than the majority of professedly pornographical books. James Joyce sticks at nothing, literally. He forbids himself no word. He says everythingâ everything. The code is smashed to bits. Many persons could not continue reading Ulysses; they would be obliged, by mere shock, to drop it. It is published in France, but not in French, and I imagine that if it had been published in French there would have been trouble about it even in Paris. It must cause reflection in the minds of all those of us who have hitherto held and preached that honest works of art ought to be exempt from police interference. Is the staggering indecency justified by results obtained.? The great majority of Britons would say that nothing could justify it. For myself I think that in the main it is not justified by results obtained; but I must plainly add, at the risk of opprobrium, that in the finest passages it is, in my opinion, justified.

ONTARIO

The greatest football match of the year has taken place, with all the usual features of frenzied partisanship and jollity. I was walking along Fulham Road in Chelsea the other Saturday with a University man, and our way was impeded by the outpouring of thousands of enthusiasts from a certain famous football ground.

Said the University man:

"It's a pity they don't play football instead of watching it!"

I said nothing; but thought much.

First, men over thirty-five usually can't play football, for good reason.

Second, men not past the football age play far more to-day than ever before in the whole history of football. There are more clubs, there is more keenness, and there is more skill.

True, professionalism flourishes, but nearly all professionals begin as amateurs, and only out of the multitude of keen amateurs can professionalism sustain itself. The huge crowds at big matches judge the game as experts, that is, as men who themselves play or have played.

The fact is, my University man had no case; he merely had prejudice. And this prejudice against the amusements and diversions and even the education of the mass of the people, though absurd and doomed to die, is still rather strong; moreover, it finds undue editorial expression in many newspapers. The kinema is derided, not because it is crude, but because it is popular. The papers with vast circulations are derided. Motor-coaches are derided. Football is derided â but not golf (despite its professionalism); oh no!

And observe the unholy eagerness with which reactionary politicians cut down the estimates for popular education.

They say the working man is not what he was. I am glad of it, for he used to spend most of his leisure in being bored. They say he does not work as hard as he did. He does not work as long as he did. When I was young I used to hear before dawn my fellow-citizens tramping in clogs to a beautiful twelve-hour day in a factory, and I used to ride in buses whose conductors enjoyed a sixteen-hour day.

The glorious past!

"Rush to the sea. Rush to the Continent." Daily papers would not be daily papers if they did not use these phrases before holidays. It must be a rush or nothing. Nevertheless, a rush there will be this week-endâ though, of course, the weather will maliciously let us down. More people go away for the minor holidays now than went for the main holiday when Victoria ruled.

And we shall be told once more that the British working-class thinks of naught but not working, and that all is changed for the worse, and that in particular the British artisan is not what he was. Well, he never was. In pre-war as in after-war days the workman's objection to work was a byword and a reproach among the employing class, and the idleness of the employing class was a byword and a reproach among the employed class. The different classes would not learn and have not learnt that no class has a monopoly of any virtue or any vice. We are all much alike in bothâ all heroes and all villains. Even the British plumber, who has been more abused than any other kind of person on earth, marvellously resembles the rest of us.

I am in favour of frequent holidays for everybody; holidays involving rushes to the sea and to the Continent. But what counts with me for good is not the reposeâ it is the change of scene.

Change of scene is the great tonic and restorer. It is also the great educator. I want half England to rush to the Continent, and half western Europe to rush to England. And I should love to see half Belfast taking holiday tickets to Cork, and half Cork taking holiday tickets to Belfast.

Every traveller is an agent of peace and understanding. A League of Universal Travel would be worth forty Leagues of Nations. A French statesman said last week that the indiscreet words of a few politicians didn't matter; the opinions of peoples alone mattered. But peoples can have no real opinions about other peoples unless they see with their own eyes. The train and the steamer are the true agents of civilisation. And the passport and the customhouse are the true foes of civilisation.

The British National Opera Company produced five grand operas in its opening week at Covent Garden, and two of them were Parsifal and Tristafi. This was a wonderful feat for an enterprise new to London. To produce even a single play, without music, amounts to a miracle, as anybody knows who has a practical acquaintance with the stage. To produce any opera is a hundred times as difficult as to produce any play. To produce five operas in five nights is just about equivalent to the whole producing work of all the rest of the West End theatres in six months. The labour of the stage-managers alone surpasses the imagination. They probably die off in dozens, but as the names of these martyrs are never advertised nobody minds much.

On the Wagner nights, which I attended, the audiences were very large and their behaviour was very good. One reason for the excellence of the behaviour was doubtless the fact that as the enterprise hasâ thank God!â cut itself off from the ridiculous and fatal patronage of fashionable, photographed notorieties, the boxes were fairly empty. Empty boxes are regrettable, but for myself, as a member of the paying public, I prefer them to boxes occupied by chattering, restless ladies who understand frocks better than decency and jewels better than manners. The audiences were artistic and earnest, with a dash of high-browism. Ah! If artistic, earnest, and high-browed women only knew how to dress!. But they don't, and it is a pity. There were not ten frocks at Covent Garden that would have passed muster at the Embassy Club. You can't have everything. Nevertheless, you ought to want everything.

You had quite a lot at Covent Garden last week. The chief thing I personally took away was the conviction that a democratic troupe actuated by courage and common sense had gathered together the lamentable ruins of a vast undertaking and had re-created them into an organisation at once dignified, coherent, and successful. The performances, though suffering from our common imperfections, were certainly better than the Covent Garden average, and in some respects far better than many perfor-mances that I can remember in the legendary pre-war grand seasons, and incomparably better than nine performances out of ten at the Paris Opera.

I was talking critically to a member of the committee, who asserted that the management would welcome criticism. This I denied, having yet met but few members of the theatrical profession who had honestly the slightest use for straight, serious criticism. However, trusting to the good faith of the distinguished member, I will here give frankly the views of a profane and uninstructed person not merely about the performances but about Wagner. Thirty years ago, when I used to sit almost by myself in the upper circles of Wagnerian opera, I would have assassinated anybody who uttered a word against Wagner. Such youths as I was probably exist to-day. My will is made, and I am ready.

Parsifal is a bad opera. The foundation of an opera is the libretto, and not millions of semiquavers of fine music will make a good opera out of a bad libretto. The libretto of Parsifal is bad. The story is poor, and there isn't enough story. It is unconvincing on its own plane. It is clumsy. Some of the most important parts of it are narrated instead of being enacted. And the narrations themselves are unconvincing, because they are addressed to peoplewho obviously must have been familiar with the facts. They remind one of such speeches in bad plays as: " Your dear mother who died ten years ago of typhoid in this very room." And they are ineffably tedious. Gurnemanz is perhaps the most boring role ever written bya genius. Further, the libretto is pretentious. Wagner wanted to beat the Gospels, and deservedly failed, from lack of inspiration. I admire nerve, but not ' impudence, and the feet-washing and feet-drying scene between Kundry and Parsifal is senile impudence.

A friend of mine said to me: " He tried to make an opera out of a mass."

So he did. The chapel scene is very effective theatrically, but it is effective only through an association of ideas; it is a stage-exploitation of centuries of religious feeling. Having got this effect in the first act, Wagner might have shown the wit to leave it alone. But no. He could not resist imitating himself at the end of the opera. How one shakes with resentful apprehension when the holy casket is funereally borne forward by the acolyte for the second time!

Klingsor is about as authentic as a Chinese juggler at a music-hall, and the short magic castle scene serves no real purpose in the story; it simply shows that Wagner had not repented the absurdity which he earlier committed in creating Erda. Nor is the music, save here and there in some glorious passages, a great deal better than the libretto. Lots of it is inflated tushery. I have always thought so, and now I think so more than ever. There were moments, there were quarters of an hour, when I was so excruciated by the show that had I been a soprano I should have screamed. My poor Gurnemanz, I dreadfully sympathised with you, babbling in the middle register your endless banalities.

All this is naught against the British National Opera Company, whose production was somewhat better than the last Covent Garden production of Parsifal, through much of which by the mercy of Heaven I was permitted to sleep. But the later production was not strikingly better. It was not at all inspired. The chapel " set " was the old one, and the garden " set " nearly as bad as the old one. The strident colours of the garden scene would have brought the house down at the Coliseum. The costumes of the maidens (who sang lovely music admirablyâ most admirably) were like nothing on earth. The entrance of Kundry, dressed like a Byzantine empress, perched on a rolling verdurous sofa that rolled to and fro at every touch from her or Parsifal, was the absolute ne plus ultra of bathos. Such matters are not details. They are of immense importance. Nor have I mentioned, nor will I mention, the worst of them.

We were asked not to applaud. Well, I didn't. Yet at the end I would have applauded the good in the performance had I not been shoo'd down by the faithful. Why should I not applaud Parsifal if I may applaud Fidelio and Don Juan and Tristan? To the statement that Parsifal is a " sacred festival drama" my answer is. Fiddlesticks! It is a mediocre opera, spuriously raised into a super-opera by Wagner's dodge of confining it for so many years to Bayreuth, that

Mecca of musical high-brows and snobs. I think that the British National Opera Company has lacked humour here, also a knowledge of human nature. And let me mention that on the programme there is a " special notice," applying to all performances of the season, earnestly requesting all persons to be " in their seats at least ten minutes before the commencement of each act." And such hard seats, too! I am a devotee of opera, but I go to opera for artistic emotions, not to do penance.

Tristan is a very different matter from Parsifal. The story is a great story, and admirably plotted out. It is of such heroic proportions and style that the heroic physical presences which nearly always go with fine dramatic singing seem somehow to fit it and even to set it off. The moments of tedium are rare. The music is sublime, and as decade after decade vanishes backward it grows in sublimity. Indeed, Tristan has no fault save that it is an hour too long for human physique. Except Rheingold, all Wagner's operas are an hour too longâ and some of them an hour and a half too long. The Weary Titan made a point of wearying others. He did it on purpose. His original idea was to tell the story of Siegfried in one opera of about four hours. But he soon saw that such brevity would never do and, having expanded the tale into four operas, was so reluctant to bring the last to a close that he managed to turn it into a calamity. After The Twilight of the Gods the spectator leaves the theatre a broken mortal, humbly acknowledging in the composer a destroyer.

Friday night with Tristan was emphatically a night! Eugene Goossens demonstrated throughout the difference between conducting opera and wielding a baton. The singers did not begin too well, but they were soon rallied into real distinction and they ended grandly. Parsifal and the performance of Parsifal were wiped off the map. The production of Tristan, however, left me desiring something else. The scenery was new to London, specially designed by Mr. Oliver Bernard. I thank Mr. Bernard for having got away from the eternal Wagnerian green. I admit that he tried to smash an exacerbating convention and almost did smash it. But I do not think that he achieved anything more valuable. In certain minor details the ship did suggest a ship. The after-cabin, for example, appeared to have portholes. But in its main contours the ship did not suggest a ship; it did not suggest anything, unless possibly the internal decorations of a German liner, and the incredible craft was continuously sailing straight out of a back-cloth as solid as the side of a house. The colouring was, to my taste, extremely offensive I prefer the old Wagnerian ship.

In the garden scene of Tristan Mr. Bernard employed black curtains, but upon what system or with what aim I could not discover. I can conceive Gordon Craig or Lovat Eraser making an unrealistic and yet satisfying garden out of black curtains. But neither of these artists would have mixed up a new and daring convention with Royal Academy realism as Mr. Bernard does. On the right you had a range of black curtains, and against the foremost curtain a huge blossoming bush, of which Tristan in the intervals of caressing Isolda might have picked off every blossom. On the left you had masonry of which the marvellous mortar was rendered with a conscientious realism that Frith would have envied. And so on. The total result, over-lighted as it was, like all the scenes, deafened and maddened the eye, and instead of listening to the music you listened to the scenery or peered vainly into the mysterious psychology of Mr. Bernard. Not that I am unsympathetic to Mr. Bernard's intentions. I am not. Only he is an enigma to me. And in especial I failed to understand why, if he had the slightest control over the superlative switchboard of the theatre, he sometimes permitted his shadows to slant towards, and not away from, the source of light.

In other respects also the production showed a baffling mixture of realism and outworn convention. The sailor's song sounded almost exactly as it would have sounded at sea; so much so that you couldn't catch a word of it. But a little later on we had Brangaena listening to the thunderous vocalisations of Tristan and Kurwenal (whose every syllable could be heard in the farthest gallery of Covent Garden) and Isolda sitting within a few feet of her; and then Isolda asking Brangaena what the man had said! It is this kind of effect, so easily avoidable, that shatters illusion and impairs the persuasiveness of even the greatest music. Similarly, in the garden scene the wondrous distant phrases of watchful Brangaena were precisely as clear and loud as the passionate accents of Isolda and Tristan.

While eagerly granting all the acute difficulties and all the positive achievement of the new enterprise, I do insist once more that the matters upon which I have animadverted are not unimportant details. I do insist that in their untruth and ugliness they militate grievously against the conveyance of truth and beauty which the composer not quite unreasonably hoped to attain. What the B. N. O. C. needs is an expert stage-director equally versed in all the arts (except music) which are brought into play. If such a man had only half the exquisite sense of beauty which Eugene Goossens shows in rendering the orchestral music, opera at Covent Garden would develop instantly into a new phenomenon. And, finally, I reiterate my admiring sympathy with the young and delicate plant, the B. N. O. C. If I have criticised, I was encouraged to criticise. Moreover, if I didn't admire I wouldn't criticise.

The Social Butterfly

Nina, the heroineâ or the villainessâ of my play, The Love Match, is meant to be the type of the social butterfly of our day. On the first night (I am toldâ I was not present) the play was received by an exceedingly distinguished, fashionable, and variously smart audience with steadily diminishing approval, until at the end of the fifth act a well-bred silence expressed more terrifyingly than any manifestation of noise could possibly do a final and total disapproval. (Subsequently, audiences behaved differently.)

The play may be badâ I will not seek to defend it qua playâ but I have never yet known a merely bad play to be received in silence, or to get a unanimously bad Press. With an author's vigorous self-complacency I attribute the attitude of the first-night audience, and perhaps also of the Press, to a cause unconnected with the demerits of the production. (And let me interject here that I do not impugn the sincerity of the attitude, nor have I any quarrel with dramatic critics on the score of lack of sincerity. I know many of them personally, and though they may be misguided, I am convinced of their intention to give the author a square deal.) I attribute the aforesaid attitude to my treatment of Nina, the social butterfly.

It is a realistic treatment. The delicious and naughty chit remains much the same at the end of the play as she was at the beginning. She is sensual; she is an adulteress; she is greedy for pleasure; she is selfish; she is vixenish; she is capricious; she is a waster; she is ruthless; and she is charming. She goes through some startling experiences, and onceâ once onlyâ she behaves well. But she does not learn her lesson. The last curtain falls on an unreformed Nina, and there is no telling whether later on she may not drift into the divorce court a second time.

Now if towards the end I had changed the fundamentals of her character, if I had converted her to righteousness, unselfishness, steadfastness, industry, and a sense of social duty, the play would, I think, have won sympathy; it might conceivably have been acclaimed with some of the warm praise which was bestowed upon the heroine's really lovely frocks. But it happens that I was " out," incidentally, to preach a sermon against our Ninas, and I could not vitiate my sermon by letting miracles occur on the stage which do not occur in life.

For years the phenomenon of our Ninas has been impressing itself more and more deeply upon me. I have drawn the Nina, or tried to draw her, several times already. There is another Nina in another play of mine, Body and Soul, but she is not the heroine thereof. And I may invent several more Ninas before I expire from the shell-shock of terrifyingly silent first-night audiences.

In regard to the current Nina, far from accusing myself of hyper-realism in my portrayal of her, I know in my heart that I have been too indulgent towards her; and I imagine that anybody who is in a position to compare my Nina with the genuine Ninas will agree with me on that point. However, a truthful and complete portrayal of a genuine Nina would simply not be tolerated on the stage. It would either drive the audience out of the theatre or it would cause the audience to wreck the theatre, for even the smartest and most cynical persons cannot bear too much realism about charming creatures with whom they associate. The truth has to be watered downâ say two teaspoonfuls in a wineglass of Hjo. And one must be careful not to shake the bottle.

If you have the entree to certain haunts of diversion â and the entree may be had by almost anyone with correct clothes and a little moneyâ you can see lots of Ninas any night in spring or autumn between midnight and two a. m. In winter and in summer you can meet them in such cities of the plain as Cannes or Deauville. They are pretty; some are beautiful. They are as a rule of good family. They are admirably dressed, regardless of expense. They can, when they want, display a powerful charm. They dance exquisitely. They can chatter on any subject from politics to gambling much better than the most gifted parrot. They play games very well. They show positive genius in the craft of self-advertisement; their portraits appear oftener in the papers than those of stage stars, and ten times oftener than those of the admitted benefactresses of this isle.

They draw attention to themselves by fair means or foul wherever they go. Some of them are married, some of them unchaste, some of them half-virgins, and a few virgins. Some of them cadge for loans of money. Some of them continually and notoriously get drunk, and some can consume wonderful quantities of alcohol and remain sober. They are all avid of every expensive pleasure, and they live for naught else. They have never worked with a pure motive for the common good, and they never will. They grab at everything and give nothing. They are convinced that in condescending to dwell among us they have earned the gratitude of mankind. They know themselves to be the salt of the earth.

I do not blame them. No doubt they serve part of the eternal purpose, but what part I cannot guess. If censure is due it should fall mainly upon the men whose possessive vanity renders their orchidaceous careers possible. I content myself with asserting their existence and their characteristics. Of course, there have always been Ninas, but many generations have passed since Ninas flourished so astonishing and so disturbing as ours.

The Nina in my play is, indeed, but a timid and very bowdlerised version of the authentic actual Nina. And yet she is held to be so detestable that a first-night audience simply could not bear to see her unconverted to some sort of righteousness at the end of the play.

Tea on the Stage

I have never burst with pride over my plays. On the contrary, I always listen with meekness to the tale of their bad qualities: which tale the newspaper Press has always in clear and authoritative tones recited to me. In my meekness I was astonished the other day, when making certain calculations, to find that the average number of performances throughout the world of all my plays produced for a run in the West End of London was over 800â not counting unauthorised performances.

I felt a sensation akin to pride at the further discovery that Press opinions about my plays improved with the passage of time. The Great Adventure was vainly hawked round the West End for nearly two years before Granville Barker accepted it. (Several managers wanted me to alter it; I refused.)

It had a very carping and indifferent Press. But now the very papers which damned it refer to it as a wonderful play, regretting that I should have fallen so far beneath the standard of it as to commit that tasteless and feeble crime, The Love Match. (The same thing happened to The Old Wives Tale, which had a mainly rotten Press, which the English publisher allowed to go out of print, and which no American pubhsher would touch at all.)

I doubt not that in ten years' time Press critics will be writing, apropos of my Don Juan: " It is regrettable that the brilliant author of The Love Match should have descended so low as to string together this puerile and unpleasant trash."

Nothing that I have written (except The Truth About an Author) ever had such a unanimously anathematising Press as The Love Match. I am accordingly subdued. But the attitude of the latest critics encourages me to think rather better of the play than I did.

When a play about a woman causes people, especially women, to be angry, inaccurate, dis- ingenuous, there is probably something sound and vital in the play. I see from the latest criticism that the tendency is to defend my vicious heroine Nina.

First of all, she didn't exist, and never could have existed. Now she is permitted to exist, but if she sinned her husband was a cad. Moreover, the mean beast expected too much from her. Good tea, for instance! Not that the misused creature could not make good tea. Of course she could make good tea, and I was very wrong to suggest that she could not.

I must here interject that critics were unfortunate in introducing the subject of tea. Quite apart fron The Love Match, tea is pre-eminently my own subject. I will undertake to make better tea myself than nineteen housewives out of twenty in this country. I will go further, and assert that in all my life I have not met ten women who understood the mighty subject of tea, nor twenty who knew good tea from bad. Practically all tea-hostesses will say to you:

"Do you like yours weak, or shall I let it stand a little?"

Innocence! Ignorance! They might let tea stand for an hourâ it wouldn't be any stronger; it would only be more stewed and more poisonous. On the other hand, if it is poured out too soon it will only be underdrawn and powerfully indigestible. Ceylon or Indian tea ought to infuse for five minutes, and China tea for ten. After that the tea-leaves ought to be removed from the teapot. But how many housewives adopt the simple device by which the tea-leaves can be removed? Not one in a thousand.

So much for tea! And so much for the accuracy of critics. For it does just happen that there is not a word about bad tea in my play. The husband does not take Nina to task for bad tea. He takes her to task for her inability to handle human beings and her inability to keep accounts. And he is absolutely justified in doing so.

These inabilities in a wife cannot be defended. And there are tens of thousands of housewives who have never taken the trouble to get rid of them. An immense proportion of housekeeping is grossly amateurish, and this is notoriously true of Nina-housekeeping.

It should not be true of any housekeeping. A wife ought to be a professional housekeeper, just as her husband is a professional financier, or bookmaker, or archbishop, or journalist, or bus-conductor.

This is by no means the chief lesson of my play; but it is one of the lessons. No amount of sneering at efficiency will lessen its force. And to attempt to answer it by pointing out that men don't take girls to the altar or the registry office because they are good cooks is merely silly.

Obviously, they don't. Nor do men espouse girls because they brush their teeth. Reviewers

I HAVE had in my life two really bad reviews. One was of Anna oj the Five Towns. It ran thus:

"This is an entirely uninteresting tale about entirely uninteresting people." It said that and it said no more.

The other was of Mr. Prohack. It ran thus:

"Arnold Bennett's new book is very disappointing. I have just finished it, and am sorry that I wasted the time on it. My disappointment is all the more keen because his previous books were so delightful." It said that and it said no more.

Now these reviews are really bad, not because of their severity, but because they are so distressingly short. Sympathetic young authors have sometimes told me that in their opinion there was a vendetta in the Press against H. G. Wells and myself. I do not think so. Having been a reviewer on a considerable scaleâ I once reviewed about a thousand novels and other books in three yearsâ I know how reviews arc done, and how they come to be what they are. I understand the mentality of the reviewer. And

I do not believe a bit in the general vendetta, though notoriously individual vendettas are not rare in the London Press.

It makes no matter, anyhow. Nineteen reviews out of twenty, favourable or unfavourable, can have only one valuable quality, length. If they give space they are good; if they do not they are bad. Their critical estimates are worthless, both artistically and commercially. For example, I would far sooner be castigated by Mr. Clement Shorter in a page than belauded by him in ten lines. At most 5 per cent, of reviews have some interest for the creative artist. Nevertheless I am convinced that the majority of reviewers are honest fellows. The mischief with them is, first, that they are rarely qualified for their job, and, secondly, that their editors treat them hke dirt, not only sweating them disgracefully, but even refusing them adequate space in which to swing the cat. I was astonished at the Press praises of Mr. Prohack. Never have I had such a Press. Mr. Prohack got a hundred times more approval than The Old Wives' Tale. What interested me chiefly in the 95 per cent, of them was the characteristic British undertone of disdain for my alleged " efficiency." Thus:

"If he had not had so fine an efficiency he might have had a talent of the very first quality, if not genius. He has, however, modelled himself so well to good craftsmanship in writing that one almost gives up hope now of having him ever drift into the accident of being a genius."

Again:

"He is so extraordinarily efficient a writer that you quite despair of him falling into genius, although you often feel he could."

These extractsâ and I could quote more if my damnable efficiency would let meâ are very precious indeed.

Autobiography

Lewis Hind, once Editor of The Academy, published a book of reminiscences called Authors and , in which he has consecrated some space to myself. I have not read the book, nor do I expect ever to do so; but I have read many extracts from it in many reviews of it; these extracts, by their charming inaccuracy, gave me the desire not to read the book. Lewis Hind (a friend), with Hamilton Fyfe (another friend), has been responsible for the great journalistic legend, still growing yearly and now at least a dozen years old, which credits me with being the " business man of letters," and also with being the man who always succeeded in doing what he said he would do. I am not a man of business. If I were I should not pay somebody else a large annual sum for managing my affairs. As for succeeding in my carefully laid designs, the less said the better about that.

My present point is the accuracy of Lewis Hind. He wrote, apropos of my editing of the weekly paper Woman: " There was a column of Book Notes in Woman, signed May or Rosalind or Sophy or some such name, that was so good that I yearned to acquire the writer for the journal I was editing The Academy. I discovered that May or Rosalind or Sophy was E. A. B., or Enoch Arnold Bennett. A little diplomacy, a little flattery, and the dynamo me presented itself at my office for a talk."

It is true that I did write literary criticism for Woman, but the rest, with much that I don't quote, is imagination. My connection with Lewis Hind and The Academy was brought about not in the least by Lewis Hind but solely by myself. I selected some of my best reviews from Woman and sent them to The Academy, asking to be informed whether the editor would care to have that sort of stuff in his paper. He then requested me to call, and incidentally told me that what he wanted in his paper was " good nervous English." I listened to the phrase with a straight face, and afterwards supplied him with immense quantities of good nervous English. The Academy, a millionaire's toy, paid me ten shillings a column for my good nervous English, until I struck for fifteen shillings.

Lewis Hind had considerable belief in me as a literary critic, but when he heard that I was writing a novel he was alarmed for me, and said with much solemnity: " Bennett, I hear you are writing a novel. Now mark me, if you go in for it, fiction will be the rock on which you will split. You are a critic. All you critics are the same. You want to write novels and you never write good ones."

Ever amiable, ever enthusiastic about something or other, Lewis Hind showed little comprehension of literature at any time; but E. V. Lucas, Wilfred Whitten, and I, all contributors to his paper and all people with fierce convictions, managed for some years to keep him in the narrow path or fairly near it.

Night and Day at Brive

I LEFT the train at Brive. It has 15,000 inhabitants and is a busy and dusty place, a little disordered, with a good half-modernised hotel, sound food, lots of dogs, large shops, public gardens, a theatre, a church-clock that shakes the silent tower, and at night the ennui characteristic of the â province. At night you can't see the tops of the towers, but you can hear in the dark women talking sadly to each other from different bedroom windows. In the daytime women appear to be very numerous. They are enormous in girth, short, with fierce, gleaming black eyes; and conscious of themselves (by which I do not mean self-conscious in the English sense).

The church is closely built in by houses, and at the foot of it a market was held daily. Fine teams of oxen, well-groomed, strolled about almost as slowly as a ship moves along the horizon. When you watched them attentively you saw that they did move.

At the table d'hote of all the hotels the men took on, or put on, a calm air of ease, prosperity, and well-being, freeing themselves from commercial and sexual worries;

they ate and enjoyed themselves in tranquillity, as it were between two storms. At the table d'hote of the chief hotel, where the food was good, the waiters (men of the world) received remarks about it, critical or otherwise, with perfect courteous indifference; and if a dish was not entirely a success they were not upset about it. I paid at this hotel 4 francs for a room and dressing-room, I for breakfast, 3 for lunch, and 3-5- for dinner. Wine was free.

Ennui

I departed for Souillac. Half the place-names round about here seem to end in ac; but there are some that don't. For instance, I. acisque. Balzac ought to have used this name, but the magnanimous simpleton (he took Madame de Hanska seriously) kindly left it for the artificers of the following century. On the way to Souillac, as all over France, the women keepers of the level-crossings stood at attention as the trains passed, with the official staff held out stiff at right angles from the right side. All, young and old, were slatternly, and the repeated attitude grew monotonous after a few hours. They were like slaves. I saw three Biblical flails in action in various villages. When the country folk talked to me I could just understand them, but among themselves they seemed to use a 'patois incomprehensible of course. A pleasant, rather superior workman who was taking bread and wine at the inn at Gressensac, where I had tea, told me that he had a brother-in-law who was a professor of English somewhere in the United States, but his post was a poor one, because the man had no accomplishments, was no good. This workman's attitude to the professional struck me as admirable in its judicial detachment. For thirty kilometres the white road from Brive seemed always to be climbing up into the sky and disappearing there; but in all directions other than that of the road there were vast horizons. Then, round the side of a mountain, the road slipped down for several kilometres into the valley of the Dordogne and the town of Souillac. The swiftness of my descent, however, was spoilt by meeting numbers of peasants' carts on the way from Souillac. I had to slacken up in order to avoid collisions, and also I was bound to look at the carts instead of at the panoramic scenery. At 5 p. m. I ran into the last remains of a great fair; such a terrific medley of carts, horses, oxen, sheep, and dogs that I was reduced to walking, for safety. Streams of travellers were making their exit from the two ends of the town, the streets of which were capriciously and richly patterned with animal waste products. Harness-makers were busy in the side-walks. People were constantly halting to hold long conversations in the middle of the road. The standard pattern of cart was a small, longish, narrowish box on two wheels, without springs, and drawn by an ass; four or five people in each; and often the youngest woman of the party sat in the middle of the bottom of the cart, clinging hard to the seat to nullify the awful jolting, which jerked her head up with regular periodicity, and also jerked up the sides of the cart. In addition to these carts there were all manner of prehistoric wagonettes. When it began to drizzle striped cotton umbrellas rose up out of the vehicles, but certainly did not give much shelter. Astound-ingly grotesque figures of farmers and their wives; but also a few pretty girls and young women, with coiffures tied in pink ribbon. The general effect was of a mass of ingenuous simplicity, hard, poor, and common, but picturesque. I went as far as the famous Souillac bridge, much praised in guide-books. It did not seem to me to be better than a good plain bridge in excellent repair. The

Dordogne is a miserable stream here, doubtless enfeebled by the summer; several arches of the bridge were quite dry. The beggars, including an old bearded man with misshapen, shrunken legs quite bare, presented an odious spectacle of utter poverty. A donkey to match was covered with a sack to hide the collar-sores which made it twitch continually.

At the Lion d'Or, which seemed to fancy itself the best hotel, the sole waiter said, in a very Southern accent, that a lot of automohilistes had just come in a bandde and taken all the available bedrooms except one, which I accepted at one franc and a half. It was up the backstairs, and was clean, and had no other qualities. At the table d'hote, which was very good, there were, beside the automobilistes, three French families, with children well kept and silent. A very pretty girl sat next to me; she had her hair down, and wore a cheap ring; she and her mother constituted one of the families. An extreme provincial gloom impaired the effect of this excellent meal.

Tired as I was I went out into the town in search of better spirits. I have never encountered a more perfect illustration of the ennui of the province. Not a light in the mean streets, and scarcely a soul! Melancholy fell like a sinister dew over the whole place; and the ennui grew so acute that I began to enjoy it.

In front of a little ill-lit cafe, which also seemed to fancy itself the best, a girl sat dozing or dreaming at a table in the shadow of the trees conventionally flourishing out of black boxes. She followed me inside. She was the landlady's daughter, and took my order for tilleul with a slight toss of the head. As she passed the billiard-table, where a provincial blade was practising, she jolted him with intention and spoilt his stroke. They both guffawed. This was gaiety, the only gaiety. In front of a house opposite, under a raised porch, another young woman was sitting alone, no doubt plunged in the dreadful thought of the ennui of existence. The town-crier came along with his drum to announce some sort of dramatic performance. I could not believe it. He gave the tidings and departed, and in the distance I could hear him giving the tidings again. But I could not believe it. Nor did I discover the house of mirth. I saved myself with a copy of La Petite Gironde, one halfpenny, which was pubhshed at Bordeaux, and said that it had a circulation of a quarter of a milhon, and that it issued nine different editions for different departments. This wonderful manna in the desert of ennui was No. 13,213, and was dated 5th September in the thirty-eighth year of La Petite Gironde. However, it had no news less than two days old, and most of its news was three days old. But if the news had been three years old it would have enlivened Souillac. The ecstatic frogs on the Dordogne made a tremendous row all through the night.

Cries of a Ploughman to his Team of Oxen

"Herrrt! " " Olalaloo-o!"

"Teh! Teh! Tch-tch! Ten! " As if in gentle remonstrance, but loudly.

"Waâ woâ woa! " Apparently to stop them. The first three cries had no effect on the animals that I could perceive.

Shrine

The journey to Rocamadour is a series of enormous hills with corresponding magnificent descents into, and out of, various valleys of the Dordogne and its tributary the Ouisse. There is a very long climb ending just short of Rocamadour, and then you have to turn sharply and descend again. Apparently no other route exists to this place. It is one of the great show places of the department, and one of the principal pilgrim-resorts in France. Its situation is immensely theatrical, as much so as that of an Apennine village. The church is built into the rock, and the accompanying castle stands on a higher rock and overhangs the church. An old woman guide compelled me to climb to the topmost turret of the castle, and then compelled me to look down the face of the precipice, which she said had a clear fall of nearly 900 feet. Exhausted by these feats and sights, I lunched at a little restaurant where I had previously drunk milk-and-soda. I wouldn't go farther, partly because of fatigue and partly because of the singular, seductive goodnature of the dirty and blowzy waitress. The lunch was excellent, and cost two francs. The pilgrimage business is, of course, as at all shrines, commercially exploited to the full. Curio and memento shops, guides, and repulsive and ruthless beggars spoilt all the best effects; the " grottoes" illustrating in three dimensions " scenes in the life of our Lord " were ineffably grotesque. Still, on the whole, I was obliged to admit that the exploitation might have been more grossly crude, inartistic, and grasping than in fact it was. It had a certain vague decency. Perhaps the least inoffensive figures were the pilgrims themselves.

Operatic Figeac

For thirty-seven kilometres the Figeac road, which lies along a ridge about a thousand feet above the sea-level, is patrolled by savage dogs; these dogs really have to be beaten out of the belief that they own the road. The long descent into Cambat, over a perfect surface, was simply magnificent, and done at such a pace that the farm-dogs were paralysed with amazement. And then came a climb of three kilometres and more man-and-dog fights, and then another magnificent slide into Figeac. Figeac, with a small river of its own, seems dull at first, but becomes agreeable and even exciting; and the more recondite parts of it are very picturesque. In this astonishing town of 3000 inhabitants a performance of Audran's operette La Powpee was being given, with orchestra and all, by a troupe of professionals in a booth theatre. I could hear the singing from my room in the hotel. I cannot conceive any professional operatic performance in any town of 3000 inhabitants in England, or even of 13,000 inhabitants. There was much movement in front of the opera-house. A starlit night lay over the narrow streets that spread out at intervals into three-cornered or thirteen-cornered little places. Churches were endemic. Several large cafes. A sort of beer garden, where I drank camomile. Some large shops. The confectioner's shops had great mantles of pink muslin thrown over all their stock at night, and at one shop this mantle was suspended from the central lamp of the establishmentâ like a canopy over a bed full of brides-cakes. Golden youth promenading in high collars and new straw hats. In spite of the theatre and the cafes the barbers' shops were crammed with sheeted Shagpats. They always are in the South, where barbers must be sure of vast fortunes, as brewers in Anglican isles.

The next morning I went out at seven o'clock to get a shave, and was charged threepence because the day was Sunday. And now Figeac presented itself as one of the most consistently picturesque towns that I could remember. The whole town is old and rotten-ripe. High houses with red roofs, broad eaves, a top storey in the form of a loft practically open to the street; line blue shadows, a Spanish effect. Even an eighteenth-century house looks too modern in Figeac. I saw that the churches would hold the entire population at once, and that the superior retail commerce was concentrated on the river front near the theatre and the largest church, opposite which were three barbers' shops side by side. After breakfast I paid my bill at the Hotel des Voyageurs (six and a half francs, including tip, for dinner, bed, and breakfast) and set off along the bank of the Cele; then over a hill into the valley of the Lot. On the Ouisse, the Cele, and the Lot the effect of the regularly planted Venetian-mast-like poplars was to turn each river into a festive waterway. The people were abroad, in Sunday best, mild, ingenuous, polite, all talking patois, going to or from Mass. The absolutely level road grew tedious after ten kilometres of Venetian masts, and at Cajarc I recompensed myself by an immoderate lunch,â soup, boiled beef, tripe, mushrooms, partridge, cabbage, cream tarts, peaches, grapes; everything first-rate. At the meal a traveller told me with a sort of holy passion that here was the supreme country for truffles, and that the truffle harvest would begin in a week's time. I proceeded to St. Gery-sur-Lot for tea. This village is highly picturesque; I have drawn, painted, and even etched it, though after my vicious contacts with modernity I really ought to have scorned it, as subject-matter, for precisely its picturesqueness. At the Station Cafe I was welcomed, as in plenty of these tiny places, for an Englishman, and " Entente Cordiale " was a magic formula, just as a few years earlier the " Russian Alliance " had been the password into the French millennium. Here anyway is a district where eating and drinking are understood more profoundly than international politics. Having no milk for my tea, the landlady of the Station Cafe left the railroad track and slightly milked a cow for the Englishman.

The Bridge at Cahors

When I got near Cahors it struck me suddenly that the Lot had grown considerably wider. I had been following it for over sixty kilometres. Every few miles I had passed a weir. I met a few lizards, and countless butterflies all proletarian and brown. The dogs were milder in disposition. As the landlord at St. Gery said: " Everybody is very affable in these parts,â but farther south it is different." From Cajarc onwards the scenery became wilder and more beautiful; crags on both sides now, but below them still the eternal poplars without a break. The smooth, tree-reflecting river was very sinuous in wide curves; and yet scarcely a boat on the polished surface! In the whole distance I saw only three in motion, and two of them were at Cahors. As for the superb road, it had been planned and executed quite regardless of cost; it was not only embanked but tunnelled; only one hill in the sixty kilometres. Impressive, this profuseness of expenditure, especially in a country where school teachers are paid less even than in England! In Cahors the Boulevard Gambetta was full of promenaders, half of whom were soldiers and the other half womenâ some agreeable. Evidently a military city, deriving much of its importance from the great institution of conscription. Very pleasant to be in an imposing town again, after so many barbaric and gloomy burgs ending in ac I entered the Cafe Tivoli, good and spacious and Parisian, and asked for a daily paper and received it furled on a stick as in all truly chic French cafes.

The hotel I chose was not infamous, and would be regarded as marvellous in any English cathedral town; but the next time I go to Cahors I shall try another. My bedroom was large; it possessed a sofa, but no wardrobe, nor electric light. More than thirty diners at the table d'hote, including eight militaires and several ladies. One outstandingly pretty girl in an ostentatious hat.

The hat was deplorable. Also she was a spoilt girl. Still, very pretty indeed. What a pity one can't, on those tours, send one's womenkind on by trainâ luggage in advanceâ and take them out of their trunks in the evtmng, fraiches et pimpantes! On the journey itself they offer disadvantages, and as a rule the prettiest are the most disadvantageous. I noticed that the dinner was mediocre, and a bit " short," judged by the standards of the Midi. I happened to ask for powdered sugar, and was told that the hotel had none! This absence of powdered sugar preyed on my mind. It depressed me. Moreover, I was sick of touring alone. I burst forth into the streets immediately after dinner to search for the illustrious, the lovely, the unique Valentie Bridge. (Through the windows of all the hotels and little restaurants could be seen militaires and women, dining and drinking. Grade according to price.) Well may the Valentie Bridge be double-starred in guide-books! The thing was simply prodigious in the moonlight, and extremely beautiful. There cannot be another bridge to compare with the Valentie. It made me quite cheerful again, and I went back to the Cafe Tivoli and had a camomile. Each to his taste. Camomile means a clean tongue on the morrow. I paid my bill (5-i- francs) at the inefficient and unclean hotel, and left at 6.45 the next morning to make a sketch of the bridge. Q

Then I had two cups of chocolate at a cafe, and bought one pound of grapes and two peaches for seven sous, and set off therewith for Caussade. Magnificent weather, but a strong contrarious wind. The winding road climbed gently and steadily. It wouldn't stop climbing. Aware that it would in the end have to stop climbing, I said: " I won't eat this fruit till I get to the top." Unreflecting resolve! I ate the fruit at the twentieth kilometre out of Cahors. What with the sensation of triumph, and the marvellous panorama beneath me, and the refreshment of the fruit, I could not help giving forth savage and inarticulate voluptuous cries as my teeth met in the absolutely perfect peaches. I was at Caussade before noon (38 kilometres). A vast fair was in progress, and the main street was lined with a double row of serried oxen, horns facing horns and a lane between. An admirable lunch at the crowded Hotel Larroque. The service had been a little disorganised, but not the cooking. Every town has the hotels it deserves. They knew food from forage at Caussade. From Caussade I had a tremendous, an appalling climb, and a fearful series of descents into St. Antoninâ a town lost in antiquity, hills and picturesqueness, a town unknown to globe-trotters and excursionists, a town so anciently elemental that its streets bear no names and have to be described as the street where Monsieur Chose lives, etc. Yet I shot through it as though it was Basingstoke, because my destination, Fenayrols-les-Bains, was only a few miles farther on.

The Destination

Fenayrols is the local " watering-place," with medicinal springs in the bed of a stream, and a hotel. You walk out with a glass in your hands to the Source de l'Eglise, before breakfast. However slowly you walk you will pass other small moving groups, with glasses, as though they were standing still. It is amazing, the slowness which some people, especially cures, can accomplish in perambulation. Last month, August, there were forty-eight visitors in the hotel. The season was in fullest swing. Now there were only eightâ three old women, one old man, two cures, and ourselves. One of the cures is a very nice quiet fellow, bored with existence and missal-reading; only a little bored, but decisively and fixedly bored. He never goes out except to drink the water or to visit the cure of the village. Lunch occurs at ten-thirty, and the landlord presides. His name is Roucoule but I call him Roucoucoule, A jolly man, who laughs at everything, and uses the most terrible, the most impossible words, prefacing them with, "Vous m'excuserez le mot messieurs et dames " â and out the word comes. The company is intensely respectable, nevertheless, despite the landlord's vocabulary and the general table-manners. The table-manners would not bear description in English. One day the Mayor of Gaillac came to lunch, and kept his hat on throughout the meal. But that was nothing. A hat at any rate does not make a noise. During meals we talk of things and the price of things, and eating and drinking, and health. Everybody is a real connoisseur of wine. Truffles cost 17 francs a kilogramme. This seemed to me rather dear, but I was told they might cost 35 francs in Paris. (Everybody has great contempt for Parisian cookingâ and justly, for the cooking of the Midi is better, even at railway stations.) Milk costs five sous a litre;Â but some of us remember it at three sous. An old lady recalls the day when at Montauban ass's milk was a regular commodity famous for its fine taste and its curative properties. It cost a franc a litre. Now it has almost disappeared from the market. I am informed that if a healthy man is to live on milk alone he must drink six litres a day. At Toulouse milk threatens to rise to six sous a litre. So our table-talk proceeds. If it flags we take to discussing the names of things in patois, and the varieties of patois. This leads to about five new discoveries every minute.

Scenery and Character

I never stayed in any province so provincial as Fenayrols. Its contented and bland ignorance concerning matters of common knowledge is absolutely impregnable. At table I have not heard one general idea. Not one! I walked this afternoon by the river, with a companion, and beheld women standing in the water to wash clothes. They did not even tuck up their skirts. They just stood as they were in the water and washed clothes. My companion said they did it all day. I asked how they managed in winter. They did the same in winterâ and for no reason save nonchalant stupidity. In the northern parts of France the washing-stands are primitive enough, but they do keep the washer's feet and legs fairly dry. Here the populace will take no trouble. It prefers dirt, discomfort, and disease, to trouble. So much for the alleged uplifting influence of sublime scenery! The scenery of the district is astounding in its grandeur, majesty, and beauty. But you get used to it. We rode to the Chateau of Penne, which in its impossible picturesqueness, balanced on a crazy crag, has to be seen to be believed. The whole countryside is indeed dotted with vast marvels. Yet the environment does not fortify the character, nor chasten the morals, nor improve the taste; and civilisation is two hundred years behind that of rural Belgium.

Truffles and Agriculture

Still talking about truffles, an obsession! Knowing nothing whatever about truffles, save that they are delicious and indigestible, I was staggered to learn that sows are encouraged to root for them. (Sows, because the males are fattened and killed.) The sow prospects for truffles with her snout, and when she has " found " the human being comes forward with a spade and digs up the harvest, which, of course the sow never gets. Truffles have a convenient habit of frequenting the same place. They like to grow under certain species of oak. Which makes them easier to discover.

And I heard a woman on a mountain-side crying through the trees: " Beni! Beni! Beni! " (patois for Viensâ " Come "). She kept on with this cry until I saw a sow in a field lift her head and listen and then amble off, gently meandering, in the direction of the c. y. She seemed to go quite intelligently and willingly, and only stopped once to investigate the possibilities of a puddle.

Much higher up on this gigantic mountainside I met a very small cottage in a dreadful state of neglect. Was it conceivably inhabited? I turned the corner of the wigwam and saw an appalling very old woman. She sat in the open doorway at some domestic task, amid old pans, lumber, and refuse. A really horrible hag, with steely wisps of grey hair, a face spotted with warts or other excrescences, and no teeth. She was typical of the aged female in these partsâ except that she scowled at me. As a rule the people are extremely polite. Indeed politeness is the one thing that they will put themselves to any trouble about; and the characteristic phrase is " A voire plisir."' The cottage had one room and a tiny attic, with a stable attached. The walls, all cracking, were held up from total ruin by roughly cut tree-trunks. A small puddle had been formed by damming a rivulet that dashed down the steep road. The puddle looked like a puddle of yellow-ochre paint, inexpressibly foul. But four ducks found it interesting and agreeable. In the evening, when I descended the mountain, the old woman was housing her ducks for the night.

I have seen more Biblical flails in use. A somewhat clever device is a cylinder of solid stone drawn by oxen. It has a diameter of eighteen or twenty inches at one end and rather less at the other, so that the oxen are forced to go round and round in a circle. The stone is heavy enough to break up the head of wheat, but not heavy enough to crush the grain. After- wards the grain, in its husk, is put into a small hand-machine and the threshing completed. On most of the small farms in the neighbourhood there is a circular smooth place, fifty feet or so across, kept clear for this wondrous operation. Agriculture, in a great agricultural country, a country where there are nearly a million landed proprietors!

A Squire

Here have I been inhabiting Fenayrols for weeks, and I learnt only to-day that it " groans " under the tyranny of a chatelain (squire) who is exceeding rich and reactionary. Hence the clericalism and backwardness of the village. It was a tailor from the big town of Montauban who told me, and he told me with gusto. All reformers love scandals. The tailor said that there were not ten such horrid little villages in the whole of the department. Fenayrols has a state school, with a master, a mistress, ten or twelve boy pupils, and no girl pupils whatever. The children have to attend the church school. This made me feel quite at home. Although I have lived in France for years I had never heard before of a French squire. But all is not known in Paris. I believe I could find places in France where they have not yet received news of the French Revolution. Still, the squire of Fenay- rols is respected, and not everybody objects to reaction. I went along to the barber's and heard more about the squire. When I hinted at his being a reactionary the barber said calmly: " Oh, well, no doubt he has his own ideas about things."

Garlic

An invitation to tea at Madame G."s, in antique St. Antonin. Her father was a contractor and helped to build the local railwayâ such as it is. She is very old and powerful and of the purest St. Antonin blood. A wrinkled face, but with the wrinkles in good straight lines and geometric patterns like her character. A quick laugh that finishes prematurely with a spreading and falling gesture of the arms. Only her voice has the weakness of great age. She actually took me up to the second floor of her houseâ sight rarely displayed. A bedroom there was tremendously primitive: a piece bricked and boarded off from the huge attic which forms this top floor. It was unclosably open to the air at four separate rectangular apertures that would be windows were they glazed; in a storm the rain must sweep through the room. Lines were hung in various directions across the chamber; on some hung clothes, on others garlic! She said that true devotees of garlic spread it on bread like butter. An idea which affrights the imagination. " They say," she remarked suddenly, " that Paris is precisely one hundred leagues from here." A pretty thought; but she added that a league was four kilometres in that country; so that the estimate was somehow wrong. Till then I had not met the word " league " in France, except on the printed page. No doubt as the daughter of a railway contractor she thought proper to think in leagues.

Bitter outcries in the assemblage of 'petits bourgeois at the table d'hote at Fenayrols against the sinful sloth of workmen. M. Roucoucoule asseverated that it was always a couple of hours for lunch, and never more than four hours' honest work in a day. Some of them spent the whole of their energy in merely pretending to work. Fantastic stories were related of the costliness of jobs paid for by the hour. France was perishing. In former days the workman was very different. In England of course the workman still worked conscientiouslyâ that was well known. But the English were ever practical and serious. Ah! If the French. etc.

Then they talked of hydrophobia: another instance here of England's practicalness. Eng;-land suppressed hydrophobia, whereas the disease was still common in the department. Never a year without somebody being infected by a mad dog! M. Roucoucoule told of a case of a bitten man who was sent to the Pasteur Institute and cured. That was years ago. The man, however, remained obstinately in the delusion that he was not cured, and would still try to bite people if they did not show the elementary prudence to get out of his way. He was constantly warning people to keep their distance. And yet he was quite cured; he would admit that he behaved absurdly; but he could not help it. He had become incurably addicted to feeling dangerous to life.

Stained Glass and Pilgrims

We went to Caylus this afternoon, following for some distance the soft and rural valley of the Bonnette. It seemed incredible that this weak trickle of a stream should only a few years ago have flooded St. Antonin, so that Madame G."s bed was afloat in her bedroom and she had to leave her flrst floor in a boat. Caylus is a hill town, rendered illustrious by its church. As we entered the town a woman was performing a small child's toilette in the middle of the street. A little farther on we bought a marvellous peach and a pound and a half of grapes for one penny. The church was in almost perfect preservation, with stained glass among the very finest in France. The contrast between the lovely and elaborate opulence of a church's interior and the squalid, mean, ugly existence that proceeds nonchalantly outside it was specially marked at Caylus. It was dramatic; it was even melodramatic. At one period the town must have had considerable importance. We climbed farther, to Notre Dame Livron, a place of pilgrimage, with magic healing fountain, cafes, souvenirs, priests, and a dreadful untidiness of wandering waste paper.

Riding back to St. Antonin we continually overtook knots of country people, chiefly peasants, afoot or in bizarre and crazy conveyances, with bags, bundles, and packets of food. Sometimes a man and a woman would be carrying a heavy bundle swung on a stick between them. At St. Antonin we found that the town was being entered by similar strings of persons from all directions. At a cafe the landlady told us that a grand pilgrimage to Lourdes was starting that night. The train left at 7.30 p. m. and was to arrive at Lourdes at 6 a. m. to-morrow. Return fare, 12 francs. Some excessively prudent pilgrims were taking even loaves of bread. " Suppose there should be no bread at Lourdes," they said, according to the landlady. The dull, savage, simple faces of the pious adventurers explained at once the tremendous vogue of the miracle-resort. One thought of the barbaric night in the uncushioned excursion train, and the condition of the carriages and the travellers at the end of the journey. Repulsive, humiliating.

â Grape-Harvest

To-day (15th September), round about Fenay-rols, the vendanges began. A solemnity. (At all times some 50 per cent, of the conversation is about grapes and wines, and everybody seems to an Englishman to be a connoisseur.) When I went forth at two o'clock after a shower of rain, men and women were gathering grapes in hundreds of acres of fields. And on the roads were congregated long, narrow, two-wheeled carts, oxen-drawn, with barrels in a row on them. The grapes were thrown into the barrels. I learnt that the grapes of the district were less good than usual owing to lack of sun, and also that they had been impaired by fogâ hrouillard. es was the word. At this point I brought my investigations to a close. It is dangerous for a novelist to specialise; he might get lost. A novelist who does not keep on writing the same book over and over againâ as too many of us doâ is condemned to have no precise knowledge of anything on earth.

â A Mayor

The Mayor of Gaillac came again to the hotel ordinary to-night; and again wore his hatâ extremely on one sideâ throughout the meal. He is an enormous man, very high and very fat, with pendent cheeks that almost flap; dirty, untidy, probably nearing seventy; thumbs turned well back, walks with the help of a rehable stick. He speaks with a most pronounced Southern accent, and between speeches he mumbles quite inarticulately at considerable length. He had sat all the afternoon at a table in front of the hotel, ingurgitating steadily. But he showed no sign of intoxication. At dinner he drank a bottle of white wine, and to begin with insisted that it must be sufficiently sec. If it wasn't sec he would have no use for it. By happy chance it proved to be sufficiently sec. He tasted it with the gestures of an immensely experienced drinker. He related in fullest detail how he would go after game with a stick, and how sometimes he had dogs that would hunt entirely by themselves. He was gigantically boring, to match his size. Before dinner was over he had a rival in the shape of a bald angler from Toulouse, also with a powerful Southern accent. The latter explained that as he was a fisherman he didn't care for the taste of fish. His leading subject was local avarice. He had an employee with no relative nearer than a second cousin, who deprived himself of nearly everything except Hfe in order to save. The fellow was positively worth 150,000 francs, and yet wouldn't indulge in coffeeâ no, not coffee!â and in winter he burnt old newspapers instead of firewood. The Toulousain recounted things with an irritating elaborateness. He would dramatically startle you with some statement, and then add in a quieter voice: " I will now tell you why," or " I will explain why."

Later this Toulousain was joined by a friend, also bald, and they made a pair of typical Southern French bourgeois. Their characteristics seemed now to be accentuated. And their two leading characteristics were certainly a powerful interest in food, drink, and physical comfortâ the yarns they relentlessly span of adventures in hotels and of what they had eaten or refused to eat!â and a refusal to recognise that women were women. With women they were consistently rosse, and very rosse. In particular they talked at length to two girls without even the slightest momentary admission that girls are entitled by universal usage to certain chivalries of manner and tone. Latin hardness unashamed, perhaps unconscious; but anyhow intensely disagreeable.

Medieval

We climbed to Cordes. It stands theatrically on a hill, whose final slopes were something like a ladder up into a loft. A gradient of one in one, or perhaps two in one. These slopes had to be climbed to be believed. As we approached the centre of the tovn we passed under one massive gateway after another, each commanding a sharp corner. Nearly all the towns round about are on hills and built to be impregnable against assault; but Cordes was pre-eminent among them. It was almost the oldest. It made St. Antonin and Caylus and Figeac look modern. Gothic houses with carved fronts, mediseval. It seemed to me that they might have been built for the Schoolmen and that therein Nominalists might have sheltered from the murderous attacks of Realists. But not beautiful, merely antique. The only beautiful thing I noticed in Cordes was the rosace in the church. The town, however, is a most marvellous historic monument, and apparently quite unvisited by the curious. The landlord of the cafe where we drank fine tea was a manufacturer of embroidery and wanted to show me his manufactory. I refused to see it, holding that in Cordes manufactories ought not to exist.

The Scale of Things

We travel and learn. The theatricality of Cordes and of Penne is as nothing to the theatricality of the chateau of Bruniquel; set, too, amid river scenery of the first order. The clotted picturesqueness of the whole district begins to cloy after a week or two; there is too much of it, and it is altogether too scenic. We returned to St. Antonin by train, nauseated with picturesqueness. Driving home from St. Antonin to Fenayrols, M. Roucoucoule, the hotel landlord, told us that he drove people to and from the station gratis, because if he charged he would have to pay 70 or 80 francs for a licence and it would not be remunerative. This shows the scale of things here. And I learnt also that a tobacco bureau brings in 70 or 80 francs profit per annum. And, further, I learnt that the excruciating cracked bell which wakes me every morning at 4.30 is the Angelus. It is rung by a woman at no salary. Once a yearâ or was it twice a year?â she makes a collection. Some contributors give her an egg others a sou. But when the landlord of the hotel (to her the symbol of shameless luxury) gave her ten sous, half a franc, she was not satisfied, and said gloomily: " Qa vaut bien ga!"

Omelettes, Soup, and Wines

To-day, there being a great influx of guests, the landlord constituted himself the chef, and the lunch was unusually good. The omelette in particular had a success. All the gourmets and gourmands present agreed that a man could make a better omelette than a woman. A R woman could not leave an omelette alone. She worried it; she cooked it too much, and unevenly. On the other hand, all agreed that a woman would make bouillon better than a man, because she took more care of it, skimmed it more conscientiously, and so on. I felt that all the talkers knew profoundly and passionately what they were talking about.

When these people begin to talk wines they never stop. It was a great wine-gossip day. I learnt that you can " age " wine by heating it to 75Â Centigrade, and that you can give red wine the characteristics of maturity by mixing with it 25 per cent, of white wine. Everybody agreed that the department produced fine wines, and the white wines of Gaillac were continually spoken of with high respect. A post office inspector who came in for dinner, a man of very superior education and bearing, seemed at once to establish himself as the leading wine expert of the table. He asserted that for forty francs the fiece (sufficient to fill over two hundred bottles) you could buy the very finest in the district. There was a lot of talk about the extreme difficulty, almost the impossibility, of obtaining authentic winesâ that is, wines which actually were what they pretended to be. This applied specially to champagne. As for Bordeaux, the dealers from Bordeaux came to the department, and to the neighbouring depart- ments, and bought wine freely, which was sent to Bordeaux and thenceforward was Bordeaux. The department of Tarn-et-Garonne was famous for its excellent Bordeaux! The inspector said that most of the great brands were farmed out, and the money had to be paid whatever the yield was. Hence a certain quantity of Chateau Blank simply had to be found each yearâ from somewhere! He showed why the dodge of selling the yield " on the vine " sur pied) was so tempting to the vine-grower. He said that there were scarcely any pure French wines left, Californian plants being grafted on to everything. I understood that at forty francs the-piece wholesale, the grower can make a good living; at thirty francs profitable business becomes difficult and uncertain. Of course the general conclusion was that the vineyard industry was in a bad way. In France, as in England, it is rare to meet a man of business who does not anticipate ruin within a few years.

The Hotel Staff

The waiter left unexpectedly this morning, a week before his time was up, having found a place in a cafe at Toulouse. The landlord was not in the least disturbed. Pauline is now cook, chambermaid, and waitressâ with often a dozen or more at table. She manages quite well. (Oh, country hotels in England!) My mature impression of Mr. Roucoucoule's establishment is that it is a very sound proposition at six francs a day. Good table and too much to eat. Excellent wine. Cleanliness fair. Sanitation fair.

Service quick and willing, but a little slow at meals, which are not always prompt; everybody genuinely anxious to oblige. No extras. No attempt to " make a bit." Large rooms. Simple but just adequate furniture. No carpets, unless you count bedside rugs as carpets. Not a doormat in the place. Too many flies.

Blasco Ibanez

I made acquaintance with the work of Blasco Ibanez. A novel translated by Herelle (the gentleman who kindly adapted d'Annunzio to the French taste), and entitled in French Terres Maudites. It opens with an extremely competent full-dress description, in the Zola technique, of the beginning of a day in the huerta (Valencia region). Then the theme of the story is well stated and the dramatic situation well presented. Your interest is aroused. And your interest is soon disappointed. The construction, if any, of the book is rotten, a regular mess being made of the most magnificent material. Much prominence and much space are given to the figure of Pepita in the first chapter. You are justified in assuming that she is the heroine. Well, she has nothing whatever to do with the main story; she disappears. " My God! " the author must have said to himself towards the end, slapping his thigh, "I've clean forgotten that girl Pepita! " And Pepita is dragged in by the hair for the finale, which finale is quite unconvincing. If Blasco Ibanez had had any power of self-criticism, or in the alternative any artistic scruples, he would have ripped the novel up and started it afresh. Further, he is terribly sentimental. His admiration of the peasant " colossus " or " Herakles " is naive to the last degree, and reminds you of the worst quahties in Camille Lemonnier's once semi-famous but totally ridiculous novel, Un Male. I should say that Blasco Ibanez was young, and also that he would never do anything first-class.

The Station Staff

The landlord told me that the railway station of Fenayrols is manned by one woman, who does everything. She shuts and opens the gates at the level crossing, works the signals, deals with the goods-traffic, sells tickets, collects tickets, cleans, and keeps the accounts. Passengers are compelled by by-law to help her with heavy luggage. Two years ago she was paid thirty francs a month; she now gets fifty francs. Her husband is head platelayer for this section of the line, and earns eighty francs a month. In summer she is grossly overworked. But in winter, the landlord positively assured me, " sometimes not a single passenger alights at Fenayrols in a fortnight."

Stone-breaking

We talked to an old stone-breaker on the road. He said he had lost his wife, son, and daughter-in-law, all in the last nine months, and now lived quite alone at St. Antonin. He had fought in the war of 1870. For each heap of broken stones he received thirteen sous, and by good work he could do one heap in the morning and another in the afternoon, making twenty-six sous (thirteen pence) a day. " It's not bad," he said, pleased with his situation. But he had to walk over three miles each way to and from his job. " That's nothing," he said. " If you knew how I used to have to walk when I was young!"

Finance of Maize

Finance from old Madame G. On one bit of ground of rather more than half an acre she grew maize this year, and sells it for sixty francs. She paid two francs for seeds, fifteen francs for two and a half days' male labour, and two francs to a woman for something that I can't remember.

Thus she gets forty-one francs profit, but from this must be deducted the value of her own labour and the cost of carrying the harvest into town. As for her grapes, she cannot find men to gather themâ at an economic wage. She said to me, with a curiously dry and cynical accent: " Do you know how much they get? Well, three francs a day, and fed!. And wine selling at three halfpence a litre! " Here is the sort of reasoning that confounds publicists.

The Truth about Fenayrols

It takes me a long time to put two and two together. After I don't know how many days, I now account for the undeniable backwardness of Fenayrols, not by its reactionary squire, but by the fact that it lies nearly a mile off the high road along a by-road. The by-road, however, is fairly good up to Fenayrols. Beyond, lie a few miserable hamlets, which doubtless regard Fenayrols as a sort of metropolis. After that nothing in particular that I could find. The metropolis has a few hundred citizens. There is an iron bridge over the beautiful Aveyron. The church is half a mile off, but a small chapel with an angelus-ringing belfry exists in the village itself. A small market-square, with municipal flowering plants and a vine or so; a small town hall with a small tower; a post oflbce. The post office, strange to say, is both clean and well run. The most marked characteristic of the whole place is animal excreta. The pools and puddles which the ducks eagerly explore are so marvellous in morbid decadence that, had he known them, Clement Scott would certainly have employed them metaphorically when discussing Ibsen. Most of the houses are far gone in decay; some of them look as if they had not been inhabited for quite a century; but they are inhabited. Structural repairs, if any, are of an extremely makeshift kind, and very amateurishly executed at that. All the lanes are merely tracks of loose stones. We have two grocers, and several other tiny shops, a cobbler, and a barber (clean) who is also the tailor. Lastly, there is a second hotel, not comparable to our huge caravanserai at six francs a day inclusive. Somewhere in the lanes is a weaver who works on a primeval loom, and I hear of a carpenter.

Discuss the village with the landlord of the huge caravanserai and he has only one important theme: the rapacious, self-defeating narrow-mindedness of the peasantry. They think that he ought to pay more than other people, and, rather than sell to him at current prices, they let him buy all his provisions at St. Antonin. They do whatever is possible to make the running of the hotel difficult. The squire is the chief shareholder of the company owning the hotel.

(I am modifying my opinion of that mysterious reactionary, for he is very well-spoken-of by everybody in the village. His chateau has a forbidding and ruinous exterior, but I am told of wonderful Louis Quinze furniture therein, including a drawing-room suite embroidered with the fables of La Fontaine, for which sixty thousand francs has been refused.) Several companies have preceded the present oneâ and failed. One of them spent eighty thousand francs on building an etahlissement on the banks of the Aveyron, and the Aveyron ridiculously overflowed and wrecked it before it had brought in a cent. The increasing frequency of great floods renders its restoration impossible. The only thing to do would be to build again at a more respectful distance from the river,â and who is going to start on such an adventure? The company pays five hundred francs a year for the monopoly of the medicinal waters. The inhabitants of neighbouring communes have the right to take water from the springs for their own use, but not to sell it. However, they sell it, and the company is still trying to find a way of stopping them.

A Great Restaurant

Vaour is a village I don't know how many miles off Fenayrols. I only know that we went there, and it lies eleven kilometres from a railway station. The Hotel du Nord at Vaour is illustrious throughout the region for its cookery. People travel vast distances uphill in order to enjoy it. We did. We arrived at eleven o'clock, and lunch wns just ending. The landlord and landlady in the kitchen said that we were unfortunately too late for a proper meal, but they would see what they could do for us. Here is what they did for us:â

Soupe.

Jambon du pays.

Confit d'oie.

Omelette nature.

Civet de li vre,

Riz de veau blanqviette.

Perdreau roti.

Fromage Roquefort.

Fromage Cantal.

Confiture de cerises.

Poires.

Figues.

We ate of everything; every dish was really distinguished. I rank this meal with a meal that I once ate at the Ktoile restaurant at Brussels, once, if not still, the finest restaurant in the world,â and about the size of, say, Gow's, in the Strand.

In addition, there were three wines, a vin blanc ordinaire a vin rouge ordinairsf and a fine wine to finish with. The fine wine was fine.

The total bill, for two persons, was seven francs.

At the entrance to Vaour is a newish chateau. We learned that it had been built not very long since on the site of an old maison â not a chateau, and that it was tres chic. When I asked if the owners were in residence, I was told " the lady only." The gentleman came very seldomâ occasionally for a week-end, no more. They entertained rarely.

"Are there any children?"

"No. The lady is all alone."

This brief glimpse of an existence eleven kilometres from a railway station had a saddening effect upon me.

From Vaour we climbed still farther to the celebrated forest of Gresignes. A state forest, a very large forest, a forest with wild deer bounding in it. Suddenly we came to a clearing and a " point of view," and the forest was spread out before us in its vastness. Beyond the forest was range after range of hills. And on the horizon a faint, long, low cloud. This cloud was lofty mountains; it was the Pyrenees, a hundred kilometres away. When I comprehended what I was looking at I had quite a thrill, for till then the Pyrenees had been only a name to me. This was a day of sensations.

The Village Fete

For some days preparations for the annual f te of the village have been in progress, and five musicians arrived from Bruniquel last night. The landlord told me that for centuries it had been the custom for the squire, when a son of his had to tirer au sort for the armv, to pay all the expenses of the musicians from Bruniquel at the fete of Fenayrols. And the squire was paying them this year. The musicians arrived last night, and I met them in the dusk in the station road. There are five, including the drum. They burst into music as they entered the village, and it was good music. The Bruniquel musicians are famous in the region. They have an ensemble. The " piston " won the first prize in his regiment, and was reputed to be able to play almost any instrument. The quintet stays at the hotel till Tuesday morning. They brought with them a curious bouquet of paper flowers for the landlady. And while we were lunching in a private room two conscripts came in bearing another paper bouquet. They were so sheepish and nervous that they could scarcely speak. " We have the honour"

and they handed the bouquet to me instead of to my wife. I gave them two francs. The youth who took the money, looked at it, hesitated, and then returned thanks. At the door there was another hesitation; at last they glumly-departed, with expressions of goodwill. I thought they were not satisfied with the tip, but to-night the landlady assured me that they were well satisfied, and that their singular deportment was due merely to shyness.

Booths and swings have been erected. One booth is perched across a rivulet of animal filth, with a few boards to make a bridge. The faeces in the road have not been removed, but have been swept to the sides of the road. This was at any rate an effort towards righteousness. The musicians, after playing late last night, were abroad early this morning; they paraded up and down, and up and down, preceded by the three or four conscripts of the village carrying a large tricolour; and there was quite a crowd, which had increased at lunch-time. At 4.30 the musicians entered the special garlanded bandstand in the square for the afternoon ball. Tables and chairs had been arranged in odd corners near each little cafe. The lordly terrace of our hotel was full. Bright frocks everywhere. The ball began. More and still more bright frocks. We saw bright frocks coming down all the hills from the hill-farms. At 6.30 the musicians descended from the bandstand, and left five empty glasses behind them. The lame barber, who, in addition to being a tailor, is to-day a cafe-keeper, climbed up into the green boughs surrounding the bandstand and removed the glasses. Evidently he has the concession of supplying drinks to the musicians.

At 9.15 the scene in the square for the evening ball was what has to be described as fairy-like, though what likeness strings of Chinese lanterns and rockets have to fairies I have never understood. The acetylene-lighted swings were continuously swinging. Still more bright frocks. Many girls were covered with confetti; yet the confetti merchant seemed to be doing no business. The postman wore a new uniform, hitherto beheld of none. A shooting-saloon in charge of an old woman with a calm and cynical glance of experienced resignation was quite deserted. Some of the girls had their hair threaded with blue ribbon, and some wore elaborate belts. They pinned up their skirts for dancing. To the thick gloom of an arch of the iron bridge all the young men retired together singing loudly. In one dark corner of a lane a boy and a girl were dancing together all alone. Aged persons sat about on chairs, some of them too far off to see anything of the fete, and apparently not interested in it. A grunt or two from some animal in an invisible stable still reminded you that animals insisted on being fed as usual. The playing of the musicians had much deteriorated. Over everything a magnificent rich night, and the Milky Way strangely glittering.

We had a glimpse of the "young heir," the gentleman whose father's traditional role it was to pay all the expenses of the five musicians from Bruniquel. A fine specimen of golden youth. He had certainly been se frotter un peu a Parisf â so he was judged.

In the Train

We left Fenayrols this morning. The bill was 255 francs for two people for three weeks. The landlord would not charge for a guest whom I had to lunch, nor for a liqueur which I had once drunk. He said that we had been absent from meals several times, and that, moreover, I often ate almost nothing. The entire staff of the hotel throughout our stay was invariably in a high degree agreeable and obliging. The village was carpeted with confetti after last night, and citizens were promenading early and talking in loud voices as though publicly determined to be idle and joyous all day. At the station we got into a compartment, and lo! the reactionary old squire, a cure, and the chief local doctor, who has a great reputation for charm, goodness, and overworking! In conversing wth the squire the doctor took out his engagement book and, pointing to a column of notes, he said: " Look! I've done all that since two o'clock this morning." (It was then 9.15.) The squire was clearly a very decent fellowâ and I didn't care how reactionary and bigoted he was.

The Theological Town of Ingres

The railway station buffet at Montauban was fully equal to its illustrious reputation. Most station restaurants in France are excellent (except of course those at the Paris termini), but Montauban ranks with Nevers, and there is no restaurant anywhere in London as good as the buffet at Nevers. On the other hand the trains which carry customers to and from these marvellous tables are absurd, tragic, and fantastic. On issuing from the station we at once became aware that one single phenomenon dominated Montauban: the blinding light and overwhelming heat. A red- brick country town, spacious, exposing itself wantonly to the unbearable sun. Naturally, I went straight to the Ingres Museum. A notice said that it was closed on week-days! The concierge, however, appreciated the impropriety of sending away bredouille a foreigner who regarded Montauban as a town containing the Ingres Museum. I could find nothing that seemed very important in the Museum: pencil-sketches, souvenirs, and so on. But perhaps the heat made me careless. I can imagine an Ingres idolator leading me into a corner and pointing to a piece of paper with a few pencil-strokes, under glass, and saying to me: " You don't mean to say you can't see that that is one of the greatest pieces of draughtsmanship in the whole of Europe!" I am well used to that sort of didacticism. Also, I am a convinced believer in Ingres. Nevertheless the Ingres Museum at Montauban bored me. We passed on to the Cathedral. Cool, incredibly cool! Romanesque. I made a sketch of the interior, and it was the very hottest hour of the day. Emerging, we almost ran, as people do in torrential rain, from one shelter to another, and found fresh shade in a public garden by the river. The streets of Montauban are crowded with priests and cyclists. Above everything it is a theological town. There are two theological faculties, each of them explaining the unknowable to its own satisfaction. Round about here they feed pigs on peaches.

A Metropolis

Toulouse. â As the train stopped we could see many watchers sinisterly scanning the arrivals. Great crowds in and round the station. The passengers fell in a cascade out of the packed train. They had only one idea, to get away. They would have nothing to do with the subway; they surged across the lines between engines and escaped. Outside there were quantities of railway omnibuses. We were swept into one. Then a long wait. The municipal in-ipector of railway omnibuses would not let us start for ages.

Instantly the " feel " of a big town, almost of a capital. The station offered an imposing fagade as we drove over the bridge of the Canal du Midi, which goes to Cette. Electric cars all over the place, except in the Rue d'Alsace-Lorraine, the principal shopping street. In this narrow thoroughfare narrow open cars were tied to the tails of skeleton horses. The Hotel de la Poste had the conveniences and the mysterious corruption and the equally mysterious glances (at once servile and disdainful) of a genuine cosmopolitan " caravanserai." Disconcerting after Fenayrols and all the dark town-lets ending in ac. We went into a large store and bought a local shawl; and then to the Alices Lafayette, the centre of cafe life. Lots of large, fine, white cafes, strident with orchestras masculine and feminine, "Roumanian " or otherwise recondite. The usual fur merchants walking about with the usual lies on their glib lips. At the newspaper-kiosks several periodicals devoted to bull-fighting. Smartish cocottes walking about. A woman who sold violets presented a pin with the bunch. The flower-kiosks bore the names of their flower-girls. Sensation of a highly sexualised town, a town in which women exploit themselves, are exploited, and play a prominent part. More Parisian than Brussels or Marseilles. After a good dinner at the Restaurant Dore (3 francs 80 centimes for two) we went by electric train to the Exhibition. Admission free at night. And so it ought to be! Really the municipality ought to have paid the citizens to go in. Besides ourselves there were about six persons. The sole attraction was the Native Village, from which we refrained. But we saw an official reading a newspaper in the midst of a pell-mell of overturned chairs on an empty bandstand. And we saw the electric arc-lights glacially shining on fine trees, marvellously kept parterres, and shut booths. All very melancholy. We were back again in the centre of night-life at 8.15. The cafes and their terrasses were full. The evening papers rushed out like torpedoes. A southern effect of packed populations: a grouillement. Language evidently free. " 11 a une gueule sym-pathique, said a serious young man to two other serious young men.

Second Day. â Churches. St. Sernan. Curious effect inside. From the aisle running round the chancel you could look down through a grille and see the crypt and women therein kneeling ecstatically in front of a casket containing a celebrated relic. And in a corner, partitioned off from the rest of the crypt, the crypt custodian, an old, thin man. All this, dim and richly decorated, seen from above through the bars you were standing on, produces a strange symbolism of Superstition caged in a sculptured and gilded prison. Over the door leading down to the crypt was an inscription: " Than this place there is no holier on earth." The church is Romanesque and very fine, full of frescoes, some good, some deplorable. In the chapels behind the chancel women on their knees fervently praying, rapt, with silent-moving lips. Crippled beggars scattered about; not many, but enough to remind you that you are in the south. At dusk, the very strangely planned Cathedral of St. Etienneâ like two churches, one breaking into the other. Overpowering effect of vast arches in the gloom. Huge candles flickering in immense spaces. A few people prayingâ diminished to dolls by the proportions of the architecture. Just enough daylight left to make the stained glass faintly glow.

Then the Rue d'Alsace-Lorraine, long, narrow, straight, profound, with all Toulouse thronging at the bottom of the canyon, pushing one another off the pavements against the trams that glide along to the clatter of hoofs. Hat-shops, stick-shops, leather-shops, jewellers', magasins de nouveautes, everything rather chic. Ladies, cocottes, thousands of men all in straw hats. Suddenly we met our disappeared waiter from Fenayrols, my letter to whom with 7 francs 50 centimes for a tip had miscarried. He stood talking to us with his hat off, very meek. His humble wife had a child in her arms and another at her skirt. This was the underworld. I wanted to tell the man to put his hat on, but I didn't, not being able to procure the right tone. I was remindedâ I don't know why â of the shopgirls whom I had seen earlier than 7.30 this morning, beginning their day's work by dusting and arranging their merchandise. It was now 6.45 and the shops were only getting ready to close. The end of a devilishly hot day. These shop-girls and shopmen really lead the lives of factory-hands; but they are neat, comparatively clean, always on show, always with " company manners." Some of the shop-girls have quite a style, despite their dull black. And they move proudly. They are conscious of physical distinction and distinction of dress. Their gestures prove that they have dominion over some man. They know what they can do.

Municipal decree posted on the walls of the Capitol: That the artists of the municipal theatre shall have three debuts, and that in the last entr acu of each debut the stage manager shall come before the curtain and ask the audience for its opinion. If after three debuts the opinion remains doubtful, then a fourth debut is permitted. In the case of artists who have previously appeared there shall be only one debut, called the rentree. All debuts must take place on Sundays or holidays. The decree explicitly declares that the good taste of the Toulousain public is renowned, and that the public shall be the sole judge and arbiter.

Lightning Source UK Ltd.
Milton Keynes UK
24 September 2010

160321UK00003B/333/P